When You Trap a Tiger

Also by Tae Keller

The Science of Breakable Things

When You Trap a Tiger

TAE KELLER

Random House New York

 Published in the United States by Random House Children's Books, a division of Penguin Random House LLC, New York.

Visit us on the Web! rhcbooks.com

Educators and librarians, for a variety of teaching tools, visit us at RHTeachersLibrarians.com

Library of Congress Cataloging-in-Publication Data
Name: Keller, Tae, author.
Title: When you trap a tiger / Tae Keller.
Description: New York: Random House, [2020]
Summary: When Lily, her sister, Sam, and their mother move in with her sick grandmother, Lily traps a tiger and makes a deal with her to heal Halmoni.
Identifiers: LCCN 2018060246 | ISBN 978-1-5247-1570-0 (trade) | ISBN 978-1-5247-1571-7 (lib. bdg.) | ISBN 978-0-593-17534-7 (int'l) | ISBN 978-1-5247-1572-4 (ebook)
Subjects: | CYAC: Sisters—Fiction. | Grandmothers—Fiction. | Storytelling—Fiction. | Sick—Fiction. | Tigers—Fiction. | Korean Americans—Fiction.
Classification: LCC PZ7.1.K418 Whe 2020 | DDC [Fic]—dc23

Printed in the United States of America
10 9 8 7 6 5 4 3 2 1
First Edition

For Halmoni—

I wish you a pendant.

1

I can turn invisible.

It's a superpower, or at least a secret power. But it's not like in the movies, and I'm not a superhero, so don't start thinking that. Heroes are the stars who save the day. I just—disappear.

See, I didn't know, at first, that I had this magic. I just knew that teachers forgot my name, and kids didn't ask me to play, and one time, at the end of fourth grade, a boy in my class frowned at me and said, *Where did you come from? I don't think I've ever seen you before.*

I used to hate being invisible. But now I understand: it's because I'm magic.

My older sister, Sam, says it's not a real supersecret power—it's just called being shy. But Sam can be rude.

And the truth is, my power can come in handy. Like when Mom and Sam fight. Like right now.

I wrap myself in invisibility and rest my forehead against the back-seat window, watching raindrops slide down the side of our old station wagon.

"You should stop the car," Sam says to Mom.

Except Sam actually says this to her phone, because she doesn't look up. She's sitting in the passenger seat with her feet slammed against the glove compartment, knees smashed into her chest, her whole body curled around her glowing screen.

Mom sighs. "Oh, please, we don't need to stop. It's just a little rain." But she ticks the windshield wipers up a notch and taps the brakes until we're going slug-slow.

The rain started as soon as we entered Washington State, and it only gets worse as our car inches past the hand-painted WELCOME TO SUNBEAM! sign.

Welcome to Halmoni's town, a town of nonstop rain, its name like an inside joke.

Sam smacks her black-painted lips. "K."

That's all. Just one letter.

She tap-taps her screen, sending bubbles of words and emojis to all her friends back home.

I wonder what she's saying in those messages. Sometimes, when I let myself, I imagine she's writing to me.

"Sam, can you at least *try* to have a good attitude

about this?" Mom shoves her glasses up on her nose with too much force, like her glasses just insulted her and it's personal.

"How can you even *ask me that*?" Sam looks up from her phone—finally—so she can glare at Mom.

This is how it always starts. Their fights are loud and explosive. They burn each other up.

It's safer to keep quiet. I press my fingertip against the rain-splattered window and draw a line between the drops, like I'm connecting the dots. My eyelids go heavy. I'm so used to the fighting that it's practically a lullaby.

"But, like, you realize that you're basically the *worst*, right? Like, this is actually not okay—"

"Sam." Mom is all edges—shoulders stiff, every muscle tensed.

I hold my breath and think *invisibleinvisibleinvisible.*

"No, seriously," Sam continues. "Just because you randomly decided that you want to see Halmoni more, that doesn't mean we want to uproot our entire lives. I had *plans* this summer—not that you care. You didn't even give us fair warning."

Sam's not wrong. Mom told us only two weeks ago that we were leaving California for good. And I'll miss it, too. I'm going to miss my school, and the sunshine, and the sandy beach—so different from the rocky coast at Sunbeam.

I'm just trying not to think about that.

"I thought you should spend more time with your grandmother. I thought you enjoyed that." Mom's tone is clipped. The rain has gotten heavier, and it sucks up her focus. Her fingers white-knuckle the steering wheel. None of us like the idea of driving in this weather, not after Dad died.

I concentrate on the steering wheel and squint a little, sending safety vibes with my mind, like Halmoni taught me.

"Way to deflect," Sam says, tugging at the single streak of white in her black hair. She's still angry, but deflated a little. "I do enjoy spending time with Halmoni. Just not here. I don't want to be *here*."

Halmoni's always visited us in California. We haven't been in Sunbeam since I was seven.

I gaze out the windshield. The landscape that slips by is peaceful. Gray stone houses, green grass, gray restaurants, green forest. The colors of Sunbeam blur together: gray, green, gray, green—and then orange, black.

I sit up, trying to make sense of the new colors.

There's a creature lying on the road ahead.

It's a giant cat, with its head resting on its paws.

No. Not just a giant cat. A *tiger*.

The tiger lifts its head as we approach. It must have

escaped from a circus or a zoo or something. And it must be hurt. Why else would it be lying out here in the rain?

An instinctive kind of fear twists in my stomach, making me carsick. But it doesn't matter. If an animal's hurt, we have to do something.

"Mom." I interrupt their fight, scooting forward. "I think . . . um . . . there's . . ."

Now, a little closer, the tiger doesn't look hurt. It yawns, revealing sharp, too-white teeth. And then it stands, one claw, one paw, one leg at a time.

"Girls," Mom says, voice tense, tired. Her annoyance with Sam rarely bleeds onto me, but after driving for eight hours, Mom can't contain it. "Both of you. Please. I need to focus on driving for a moment."

I bite the inside of my cheek. This doesn't make sense. Mom must notice the giant cat. But maybe she's too distracted by Sam.

"Mom," I murmur, waiting for her to hit the brakes. She doesn't.

Sometimes the problem with my invisibility is that it takes a little while to wear off. It takes a little while for people to see me and hear me and *listen.*

Listen: This isn't like any tiger I've seen in a zoo. It's huge, as big as our car. The orange in its coat glows, and the black is as dark as moonless night.

This tiger belongs in one of Halmoni's stories.

I lean forward until the seat belt slices into my skin. Somehow, Sam and Mom continue to bicker. But their words become a low hum because I'm only focused on—

The tiger lifts its enormous head—and it looks at me. It *sees* me.

The big cat raises an eyebrow, like it's daring me to do something.

My voice catches in my throat, and I stumble over my words. They come out choked. "Mom—*stop.*"

Mom's busy talking to Sam, so I shout louder: "STOP."

Finally, Mom acknowledges me. Eyebrows pinched, she glances at me in the rearview mirror. "Lily? What's wrong?"

She doesn't stop the car. We keep going.

Closer—

closer—

And I can't breathe because we're too close.

I hear a thud and I squeeze my eyes shut. The inside of my head pounds. My ears ring. We must have hit it.

But we keep going.

When I open my eyes, I see Sam, arms folded across her chest, phone resting by her feet. "It died," she announces.

My pulse is a wild beast as I scan the road, searching for horrors I don't want to see.

Nothing's there.

Mom's jaw tightens. "Sam, please don't throw your expensive phone around."

I stare at them, confused. If the thud was just her phone hitting the floor—

I twist to look for the tiger, but all I see is rain and road. The tiger disappeared.

"Lily?" Mom says, slowing the car even more. "Are you feeling sick? Do you need me to pull over?"

I flick-flick my eyes across the road one more time, but nothing. "No, never mind," I say.

She smiles, relieved. I am never difficult. I make things easy. "Hang in there. We'll be at Halmoni's soon."

I nod, trying to act normal. Casual. Even though my heart is jump-dancing. I can't tell Mom about this. She'd ask if I'm dehydrated, if I have a fever.

And maybe I do. I press my palm to my forehead, but I can't tell. I guess it's possible that I'm getting sick. Or maybe I just fell asleep for a moment.

Really, there's no way I saw a giant tiger appear—and disappear—in the middle of the road.

I shake my head. Regardless of whether the tiger was real or I dreamed it or I'm losing my mind, I need to tell Halmoni. She will listen. She will help.

She will know what to do.

2

Halmoni's stories all start the same way, with the Korean version of "once upon a time":

Long, long ago, when tiger walked like man . . .

Back in California, in the weeks leading up to Halmoni's visits, Sam and I would whisper those words to one another. Every time I heard them, they'd give me shivers.

We'd count the days until our halmoni's arrival, until that first night, when we'd run into the guest room and curl up in bed with her, one of us on each side, like bookends.

"Halmoni," I'd whisper, "will you tell us a story?"

She would smile, pulling us into her arms and her imagination. "Which story?"

Our answer was always the same. Our favorite story.

"The one about *Unya,*" Sam would say. *Big sister.*

"And *Eggi,*" I would add. *Baby sister.* "The tiger story."

That story always felt special, like there was a secret shimmering beneath the words.

"Catch it for me," she'd tell us, and Sam and I would reach our hands into the air, clenching our fists like we were grabbing the stars.

That's a Halmoni thing, pretending there are stories hidden in the stars.

She would wait a few moments, letting the seconds swell, and we'd listen to our hearts beating, crying out for the story. Then she'd take a breath and tell us about the tiger.

The problem is, the tiger in her stories is a scary, tricky predator. But the tiger in the road didn't seem that way. I don't think it wanted to *eat* me, though I do think it wanted . . . *something.*

I don't get a chance to figure out what, because there are no more tiger sightings as we crawl through Sunbeam. Finally, we reach Halmoni's house. It's a small cottage, at the edge of town, at the top of a hill, across the street from the library and surrounded by woods.

Mom turns onto the long driveway, and we crunch-crunch up the gravel, until we reach the top.

After she parks, she rests her head against the steering wheel and sighs, looking like she might fall right asleep. Then she takes a breath and sits up.

"All right," she says, hooking her arm around her headrest, twisting so she can see both of us at once. She plasters a grin on her face, trying to be cheerful, to erase all the bickering and stress of the car ride.

"Bad news: I left the umbrellas back in California." She grins, like *Ha-ha, whoops, funny.* "So we've just gotta make a break for it."

I stare at Halmoni's home. This is the kind of place that just *looks* magic, perched up high, with almost-black ivy creeping along the faded brick walls, windows that wink in the light, and, of course, a million stairs to get to the front door, give or take a few.

It's nothing like our vanilla-white apartment in California—in a brand-new building. With an elevator.

"You want us to run up all those stairs in the rain?" Sam asks, with so much horror that you'd think Mom asked her to bathe in a pit of snail slime.

Mom forces another smile. "What's a little rain? Right, Lily?"

My answer is simple: Yes, right. I want to go inside and ask Halmoni about the tiger. But there's no such thing as a simple question in our family. This is a trap. She's asking me to pick sides.

I shrug.

Mom doesn't let me off the hook so easily. "Right, Lily?" Her smile falters, like she might fall to pieces. There are bags under her eyes and a deep crease between her brows.

This is not the way Mom usually looks. She's usually so polished, everything in the right place, everything in order.

"Right," I say.

Sam flinches as if I kicked her.

"Well, that settles it," Mom says with relief, placing her hand on the door handle. "Ready. Set—"

Then she flings her door open and flies out, throwing it shut as she starts running. She's drenched immediately, and she's not moving fast, but she's working hard—fists pumping, shoulders hunched, head tilted forward, as if she's a bull charging her mother's home.

"She looks ridiculous," Sam says.

And Sam's not just being mean. It's true.

Mom pinwheels her arms for no apparent reason, and I laugh. Then Sam laughs, and we look at each other. For a moment we're sisters, making fun of our embarrassing mom.

I want to take this moment and stretch it to infinity.

But Sam turns away, picking up her phone and its charger and tucking them into her bra, protecting them. "Might as well go," she says.

I want to say, *Stay,* but I nod instead, and then we burst out of the car.

I have never, ever felt rain like *this.* It is insistent and cold—too cold for July—and we don't even make it out of the driveway before my shoes squish-squelch and my jeans get heavy.

Sam yelps as she runs, and I yelp, too. Because it's kind of funny and kind of awful. My eyes sting with water and I can hardly see, but the ice-cold shock of rain lights up my insides.

By the time Sam and I get to the top of the stairs—panting, dripping—I've wrung all the air out of my lungs, and my heart is bursting.

Mom waits for us on the front stoop, which is nice, I guess, but kind of strange because she should open the door and go inside.

She shakes her head and frowns. "Halmoni isn't answering," she says. "She's not here."

3

"What do you mean, she's not here?" I whisper. For a moment, I panic: *the tiger ate her.* But I tell myself to remain calm.

Mom sighs. "I don't know. I don't know."

I can't tell if she's worried or annoyed; the rain runs over her eyes and lips, making her emotions blurry. I wish I knew how she felt, so I could know how *I* should feel.

Sam fiddles with the brass doorknob, willing it to turn. But that stubborn door stays shut. "So . . ." Sam stares at Mom, then at me. With her hair flat and her thick eyeliner running in black stripes down her cheeks, she looks like a wet tiger. "We just have to wait here. In the rain. For an undetermined amount of time?"

Mom wipes her glasses on her soaked T-shirt, which doesn't help much. "No. I don't think so. Hang on." She holds up one finger, then runs around to the side of the house.

"Where's she going?" I ask. I cup my hands over my head, trying to form a protective roof, but it's useless. "Where's Halmoni?"

Sam doesn't answer. We watch as Mom stops beneath the living room window. She taps the side of the pane, runs her hands over the sill, then thumps a fist right below the glass.

"Well, this is normal," Sam says, voice laced with sarcasm.

Then Mom shoves the window open. She glances over at us before hoisting herself up and tumbling headfirst into the house.

"Whoa," I whisper. I've never seen Mom do anything like that.

Sam shakes her head. "*Whoa* is right. I bet she did that all the time as a teenager." Sam looks at me like she can't decide whether to frown or laugh, and I know exactly how she feels, because picturing Mom as a teenager is both ridiculous and kind of scary. It's weird to think about Mom before we existed.

But Sam smiles, and my heart relaxes. "She probably snuck out to party with her friends."

I nod. When Sam is happy, her moon face glows, and

she looks like my sister again. I inch closer to her—just barely, so she doesn't notice.

She wrinkles her nose. "Do you think she snuck out to see boys?"

"I don't think she dated anybody before Dad." I can't picture Mom with anyone but Dad. Or, to tell the truth, I can't picture her with *anyone,* because I don't remember the time of Mom and Dad.

I can tell right away that was the wrong thing to say, though, because Sam's glow shuts off fast. She clenches her jaw and turns away. "That's just naive," she mutters.

Thinking about Dad is different for Sam than it is for me. She's old enough to remember him. When he died in a car accident, she was seven. I was only four.

"Sam . . . ," I start, but I don't know how to finish the sentence.

I used to be able to talk to her. I used to tell her everything. If this had happened a few years ago, I would have said, *I JUST SAW A TIGER IN THE MIDDLE OF THE ROAD.* I would've shouted it right into her ear because I couldn't hold it in.

"I just saw . . . ," I try again. But the locks on the other side of the door interrupt me. They sing as Mom slips them, slides them and opens the door. "Hurry inside," she says, as if we could get more soaked than we already are.

Sam and I enter, leaving watery footprints in the entryway, lake-sized puddles on the wood floor.

Halmoni's house looks like a memory. The living room and kitchen cuddle together around a purple dining table and a fireplace that doesn't work. An old grandfather clock tuts in the far corner of the living room.

On the mantel, two stone lions hug a photograph of Mom, welcoming wealth into her life. On the other side, a frog guards a photo of Sam and me, protecting our happiness. And everywhere—in baskets hung from the ceiling, sitting on countertops, stuffed into bowls—are bundles of herbs and smudge sticks, to cast away bad energy.

When I breathe the house in, the scent of buckwheat noodles, sage, and laundry detergent smells like home.

Sam's less happy. She folds her arms over her chest and frowns. "Um," she says. "What's that?"

I follow her gaze. At the other end of the living room, there's Halmoni's bedroom, the bathroom, and two staircases: one that goes up to the attic bedroom, and one that goes down to the basement. But now, in front of the basement door, there's a tower of engraved Korean chests and cardboard boxes, stacked like a barricade.

Mom shakes her head. "That's bizarre, isn't it? Why would she do that?" She chews on her thumbnail and glances around the room. For a second, I catch the worry in her eyes.

My earlier excitement drips away. It *is* odd. They're out of place. And Halmoni's not here.

Something cold and dark settles in my stomach. "Where's Halmoni?" I ask.

Mom looks at me and softens. "Oh, don't worry. I'm sure she's just out shopping or visiting her friends. You know how she is." She gives me a smile that's sad and hopeful at once. "Are you happy to be here, Lily?"

There's something going on, something she isn't saying. I want to ask her about it, but I don't want to take away her smile, so I just nod.

She's about to say something else, but a shiver grabs me by the shoulders and shakes me.

Mom blinks at us, like she forgot how wet we were. "Right. Hang on. Let me find something for us to change into." Our suitcases are back in the car, and none of us want to brave the rain, so Mom wanders down the hall and into Halmoni's room.

When she emerges, her hands are full of towels and Halmoni's silk nightgowns, and Sam and I pluck two off the top. The pale orange nightgown shimmers and shifts like sunset in my hands. Even Halmoni's pajamas are beautiful.

"I'm gonna turn up the heat," Mom says. "Wait here."

But of course Sam doesn't wait. As soon as Mom walks back into Halmoni's room, Sam dodges boxes and furniture and heads right upstairs to our bedroom, leaving puddle-lakes behind her.

I start after her, but hesitate. I don't want to be the little eggi who follows her unya everywhere. But in the end, of course, I follow her anyway.

Upstairs, the attic room is creaky-cozy, with peaked ceilings, a full-length, wood-framed mirror, and two twin beds dressed in faded quilts. When Sam and I lived here, we pushed the beds together and curled into one another, trading stories in the dark.

Now the beds are on opposite sides of the room, separated by the wide window.

Sam throws off her wet clothes, smears her dark makeup onto the clean towel, and tugs the black sequined nightgown on. Then she flops onto her bed. The mattress greets her with a groan, and she reaches behind the bed frame to plug her phone in before turning to me. "What are you doing? You were supposed to wait downstairs."

Sam always acts like Mom's orders only apply to me, which is annoying, but I'm used to it.

I sigh and dry off before slipping into my own nightgown. The soft warmth sends a shiver through me, releasing the cold in my bones. I breathe in, hoping for Halmoni's milk scent, but all I get is a hint of soap.

Sam frowns, still waiting for me to leave, but I sit on my bed instead.

"Does this place feel weird to you?" I pick at the bedspread as I speak, careful not to look at her. "With Halmoni missing, and all that stuff blocking the basement, and the . . . just the vibe? Like something's wrong?"

"First of all, Halmoni's not *missing*. She's just out. Don't be so dramatic. Second of all, yeah. The vibe is weird. But Halmoni's house always feels like this." Next to her, Sam's phone goes bright and begins loading, like it's stretching as it wakes up from a nap. She grabs it and watches it blink on, only half paying attention to me. "Do you remember last time we moved here?"

"Kind of." We lived here for three years after Dad died. I was born in California, but my first memories are shaped like this house.

Sam scrolls through her phone, and I don't expect her to respond, but she drops it and looks up. "At first it was nice to be here, because Halmoni took care of us when we were sad and she helped Mom out. But Halmoni was always doing weird things without explaining any of it. She's full of secrets. This house is full of secrets."

I chew my lip. "Like what?"

Sam rolls her eyes. "I don't know. That's not the point. The point is we're here instead of California and I hate it. I hate being here."

Sam's words are so harsh that I flinch. "Don't say that."

The way I remember it, Sam and I loved living here.

We were sad because of Dad, of course, but it wasn't all bad. Sam and I told stories in the attic room, we ate rice cakes in the kitchen, we created imaginary worlds in the basement. We were *together.*

I want to ask her, *Do you remember?*

But Sam keeps going. "It's just not fair, Lily. Mom wanted to move closer to Halmoni, which is nice and all, but we didn't even get a say. We didn't even get to say goodbye. Aren't you a *little* bit angry?"

If I'm being honest, I am, maybe, a little bit angry. But I'm happy to be here, too.

I clear my throat. Take a breath. Swallow. "I think maybe . . . you should be a little nicer to Mom." My palms go sweaty. This is dangerous territory. I don't usually confront Sam. We're sisters, and sisters are always supposed to be on the same side.

Sam rolls her eyes. "Seriously, Lily? I can't believe you're defending her."

"I just . . ." I can't get the look on Mom's face out of my head. Downstairs, looking for Halmoni, she seemed so fragile. Like, not how moms are supposed to look. I don't know how Sam didn't see that.

"You just . . . ?" Sam stares at me, and when I don't answer, she sighs. "Spit it out, Lily. You don't have to be so creepy and quiet all the time. You're being a QAG."

QAG is Sam for Quiet Asian Girl. As in, a stereotype.

As in, Sam tries so hard not to be a stereotype that she wears black lipstick and bleached a lock of her hair and says every little thought that comes to mind.

I tell her, *I'm only trying to help.* I ask, *Don't you see how hard Mom's trying?* I say, *I don't know why you're so* mad *at me.*

But actually I don't say any of that. The words get stuck in my throat. Sam's just so angry all the time, and everything I say sets her off.

She rolls her eyes again. "Whatever. You always make *me* be the bad guy, just because I speak my mind. You don't have to be so *afraid* to rock the boat, you know."

What Sam doesn't realize is that she's already rocking our boat. If I rock it, too, the boat will flip. We'll drown.

I listen to the rain beat against the roof, and I run my hand over the quilt. I say, "You should be happy. You *like* Halmoni." At least I think that's true. Sam doesn't seem to like anything anymore. Except her phone, maybe.

She shrugs. "I'm just saying. The point is: having to live here, without any friends, with just your mom and grandmother? That's a lot."

"And your sister," I say, so quiet I can barely hear myself. So quiet, like a QAG. "I'm here, too."

Sam has a sharp response ready, I can tell. But my words stop her. Her shoulders relax.

"Yeah," she says.

It's just one very small word, but she says it soft, and it opens up my heart and warmth spills out, spreading through my body, into my toes and fingertips.

"Yeah," I reply. I almost feel like I could tell her about the tiger dream-mirage-spirit thing.

Then, downstairs, the door slams open. Halmoni's home.

4

Halmoni throws the front door open with a bang and squeals, "Hello, my girls! My girls home to see me!"

Her voice travels all the way up to our bedroom, and I run down to see her, my feet pounding against the noisy old stairs.

Halmoni is thinner than the last time I saw her. Her colorful silk tunic and white pants hang looser than usual. Her jewel pendant rests in the U-shaped dip between her collarbones, deeper than before.

But she's still as glamorous as always, with her lips bright red, her hair permed and dyed blackest black. In her arms, she carries four big grocery bags, filled to the brim with food.

Mom's already at the door, dressed in Halmoni's pajamas and greeting her with questions—"Why weren't you here? Why didn't you answer your phone? Remember when I *told* you we'd be here at six? We had to stand outside! And why'd you get so much food? That's too much food!"

Halmoni just laughs. "Oh, my daughter, *so* nosy!" she says before placing her grocery bags and her knockoff Louis Vuitton purse in Mom's hands, as if Mom were a butler.

Mom frowns, but before she can protest, Halmoni sees me and opens her arms for a hug.

"Lily Bean!" she says. Her whole face lights up, and I didn't even know someone could be so happy about anything. I run down the hallway and slide into her arms, soaking up her love.

"Careful." Mom sets Halmoni's bags on the kitchen table and crosses her arms. "Don't knock your halmoni over."

Halmoni wraps herself tight around me and scolds Mom over my head. "Hush, young lady. At least *Lily* is loving me."

Mom sighs. "I do love you. That's why we're here."

Halmoni ignores this. She places her hands on my shoulders and leans back so she can look at me, grinning when she notices her nightgown. "Ohh, look at you. You are little mini-me! So pretty. So shiny."

I laugh. "Shiny?" Sam's the one who took the sequined nightgown, not me.

"Like the sun," Halmoni says, winking. Halmoni is the only person in the world that my invisibility never works on. She always sees straight to my heart.

"Halmoni," I say, pulse hiccuping as I think of the tiger, "I have to tell you something."

But Sam appears, padding quietly down the creaky stairs and hovering in the kitchen doorway.

"And my *moon,*" Halmoni says, walking over to hug Sam.

Sam stiffens as Halmoni wraps her up, but she relaxes after a moment, leaning into Halmoni, breathing in. Nobody can resist Halmoni. She's like gravity.

Halmoni pulls back and strokes Sam's white streak. "So pretty, you hair."

"No," Mom says. "Please don't encourage her. It's unnatural."

Sam glares at Mom, and Halmoni twirls the streak in her fingers. "It run in our family. I have this when I little, too," she says, winking at Sam and me.

Mom's voice is tight. "A bleached streak is not a genetic trait."

Halmoni doesn't even look at her. "And *so* fashion. Sam look like a rock star."

Sam grins. Mom takes a very deep breath.

Mom hates the white streak, but Sam refuses to do anything about it. She claims it's not her fault—that her hair just naturally grows that color.

It's a whole thing.

Halmoni turns back to Mom and frowns. "Why the girls' hair so wet?"

Mom clears her throat as she puts away Halmoni's groceries. "Like I was saying, they are wet because we had to stand outside in the rain. It would have been nice for you to, you know, *be here* when you said you would. I had to use the old windowpane trick and climb inside—in front of my daughters!"

"Always through the window." Halmoni looks at Sam and me and clicks her tongue. "She go out, she go in. Even the attic window, she climb out. You mother was a very sneaky child. So much trouble."

Mom sputters, and Sam and I exchange a glance. I don't know how Mom could climb out the attic window—it's impossibly high—but Halmoni always exaggerates like this, and it's funny to picture.

Sam bites back a smile and I swallow a laugh.

"And for that matter, you shouldn't be driving anymore. *Especially* not in the rain," Mom continues. "If you needed to get groceries, you should've waited for me to come. You need to be careful. You need to—"

"Tsst," Halmoni hisses, holding up one finger. Sam and I used to watch a TV show about a dog trainer who used an angry hissing noise to tame dogs. This is the same noise.

Mom clenches her jaw, then tries another line of questioning. "And what about all this stuff? Why are you living like this?" She gestures to the stack of boxes and furniture in front of the basement door.

Halmoni shrugs one shoulder. "The basement flood, so the stuff come up."

Sam raises an eyebrow. "You carried all this up by yourself?"

Halmoni turns to her and winks, which is typical. She doesn't feel the need to answer questions, and I don't mind that.

Mom, on the other hand, does. "No, seriously. *Did* you carry this up the stairs on your own? You know you could hurt yourself. You—" She pauses. "Where am I supposed to sleep?" When we lived here before, Mom slept in the basement, wedged in between all Halmoni's things.

"You sleep in living room, on the couch," Halmoni responds, like this is no big deal.

I expect Mom to argue, but she walks over to the boxes. "Okay, well, at least let me move this stuff. We can push it away from the basement door, and I can check out the flood damage downstairs. Sam, some help?"

Sam stares at her.

Mom sighs. "Lily?"

I start to walk over, but Halmoni grabs my wrist and pulls me back. "No, no. No moving those."

Mom blinks. "They're in the way."

Halmoni waves her arms in front of her, like she's warding off Mom's annoyance. "No, no. Today is not *auspicious* day. When I move boxes out, that is a lucky day. But today is dangerous day for spirits. We move another day."

A dangerous day for spirits. I swallow. I have to get Halmoni alone so I can ask her about possible tiger spirits.

"Moving things on unlucky days—*very* dangerous. And breaking things . . ." Halmoni closes her eyes and shudders, like she can't even imagine. "If you *break* something, oh, that is very bad."

Mom looks like she might literally rip her hair out.

Sam raises her eyebrows at me like, *Here we go again,* and backs up in the hallway.

This isn't a new argument. Mom always gets annoyed with Halmoni's traditions.

Mom grits her teeth. "That is ridiculous. What—"

But Halmoni points her finger at Mom, cutting her off. "You are not the mother. I am the mother. You no more asking questions. You go change you clothes. Why you in pajamas, anyway?"

Mom opens her mouth in defense, but Halmoni claps her hands. "I set up dinner now. Lily help me."

I didn't exactly volunteer, but Halmoni has a way of creating her own reality. Besides, I don't mind helping.

I follow her to the kitchen counter, and Mom gives up on the boxes. She grabs Halmoni's raincoat and stalks out of the house, down to the car to fetch our suitcases.

From the doorway, Sam clears her throat, and I glance back at her. She hesitates, like she's waiting for something, and I mouth, *It's okay. Go upstairs.*

I feel bad sending her away, but Sam doesn't like cooking or setting the table, or doing any chores, really, and I need to be alone with Halmoni.

Sam frowns and turns away, mumbling something about her friends as she heads back to the attic room.

When she's gone, I whisper, "Halmoni, something happened."

She tucks a strand of hair behind my ear and kisses my forehead. "Yes, little one, I want to hear about that, but first, time for *kosa.*"

"Yes, but—"

"Ah, ah, this first." Moving through the kitchen, she pulls bowls and baskets out of cupboards and sets them in front of me.

I don't remember the first time she showed me how to do a kosa. It's just something we've always done together.

We lay food out for the spirits and the ancestors and let them feast before we do. *For the ones who gone before us,* Halmoni always says.

When I was little, I used to pretend that Dad would come for kosa, to eat with us. I made the mistake of telling Sam once that the food was for him.

Her face twisted up and she spat, *He's dead. This isn't a game.*

She never liked kosa after that.

After Halmoni heats a plate of red-bean rice cakes, she hands them to me, and I arrange them in a bamboo basket, the way she taught me. Carefully, lovingly. They warm my fingers.

"This very important to do on days of big change," Halmoni tells me as she pours wine into small ceramic bowls. "When people come in. When people go out. We do this to keep spirits happy."

She leans closer, her breath tickling my ear. "When spirits are hungry . . . *almost* as scary as when you mother is hungry."

I smile. "What about when Sam is hungry?"

Halmoni's crinkly eyes grow wide. "That is *most* scary."

I laugh at Sam's expense, feeling a little guilty. Then I lay dried squid and anchovies on a small plate while Halmoni prepares the meal, and I listen to the melodies of kosa.

Halmoni hums a song I don't know, probably a Korean lullaby, and the house seems to sing along with her. The cabinets whisper as she opens and closes them, and the water whistles as she washes vegetables.

The thing about kosa—about all of Halmoni's beliefs and rituals—is that I've always taken them for granted. They make sense to Halmoni, so that's good enough for me. Her magic never needed an explanation. But now, with the tiger, understanding it all feels important.

"I saw something in the road," I tell her.

"What you see?" she asks as she chops a cucumber.

I swallow. "Um, I think I might have seen one of the . . . hungry spirits?"

She sets down the knife and turns to me. Her eyes are intense. "What you saying, Lily? What you see?"

Suddenly I'm nervous. "I don't know. . . . I guess it might've been a dream?"

Halmoni leans closer. "Dreams very important, Lily. What do you see?"

Mom would tell me not to encourage Halmoni. Sam would tell me I'm being weird. But with Halmoni, I'm safe from judgment. "A tiger."

She hisses through her teeth. "What that tiger doing?"

I know she's not upset with me, but she's still upset, and I can't help feeling like I've said the wrong thing. "Um, it just . . . stood there. Then disappeared." A full-force knockout wave of panic hits me, and I whisper, "Am I going crazy?"

Halmoni wraps her fingers around her pendant and leans down so her face is close to mine—so I can smell her milk breath. "Lily, *crazy* not a good word. Not a thinking word. You seeing truth because you are a special one, and that not make you crazy, okay?"

I nod, unsure what to think. The tiger *felt* real, but it couldn't be. And what do you do with things that feel real but aren't, quite?

"You mom doesn't believe in any of this. Her world is small. But *you* know: the world is bigger than what we see." Halmoni presses a palm against my cheek. "Now be safe, and stay 'way from tigers. Tigers very bad."

"I know. I'll stay away. Tigers eat people and stuff. It was just a—"

She shakes her head. "No trusting them, okay? They tricky, but you don't listen to their lies. You remember that."

"Yeah, I remember your stories."

"Yes, yes, stories. But maybe . . ." She steps back and tilts her head, like she's trying to make a decision. Something about her tone sounds off, not like the Halmoni I know. "Maybe there are more stories than I tell you."

I push away the plates and cutting board in front of me and hoist myself onto the kitchen counter so I'm sitting in front of her, ready to listen. I can't remember the last time she told us a new story. "Like what?"

"The tigers looking for me," she says, running her hand down my arm, lost in thought. "I steal something that belong to them—long, long ago, when I little like you—and now they want it back."

"Wait, what? This story is about you?"

"This one real. Tigers real."

I lean back. She's never told a story about herself before, and stealing from tigers doesn't make sense. Yesterday, I might not have believed her words. I might've thought she was just making this up, because of course it can't be real.

Just like a disappearing tiger can't be real.

And yet.

I tug on one of my braids. "What did you steal?"

If this story *is* real, maybe the tiger is, too. And maybe this is why it appeared. But what could be so important that tigers would chase it across the world? And what would it feel like, to steal from tigers—to do something so powerful and so dangerous?

She frowns. "Not important, little one. Not safe to ask too many questions."

"But—"

The door bangs open again and Mom huffs and puffs back inside, thunking two suitcases on the floor.

"No *but but but*," Halmoni tsks at me. "We don't talk about that."

Mom pushes her glasses up on her nose and catches her breath. "Talk about what?"

Halmoni gives me *shhh* eyes, and I don't say anything.

Mom blinks. "Do either of you want to tell me?"

Halmoni says, voice too sweet and innocent, "No, I pass."

Mom tilts her head. "You . . . pass? On what? Telling me?"

Halmoni smiles and nods. "Pass."

Mom looks back and forth between us, and I shrug like I know nothing.

Mom seems like she wants to ask more, but she just sighs. "Okay, well, I'll go get more of our stuff. Lily, no sitting on the kitchen counter," she says before heading back down the stairs.

I slide off the counter, but as soon as Mom's gone, I turn back to Halmoni. "What did you take? And why? And what happened?"

Halmoni hands me a stack of plates. "Enough of that. You set table now. Kosa help keep you safe. Make tigers stay 'way." She turns away from me to finish chopping vegetables.

Normally, when we set up kosa, she'll sneak me a bite

to eat early, winking and whispering, *Eat fast, so the spirits don't see.*

But tonight the mood is different. She doesn't offer, and I don't ask. I do what I'm told and set the table, thinking of tigers and thieves and Halmoni's stories.

Because Halmoni's always told us stories of impossible things, and now I wonder: What if they're possible?

5

Let me tell you a story. The story. The tiger story. In case you are wondering. In case you are sitting, waiting, wanting.

Long, long ago, when tiger walked like man, two little girls lived with their halmoni in a small vine-covered cottage, at the edge of the village, at the top of a hill. They were sisters, with long black braids, and they shared everything together, including a love of rice cakes.

One day, the halmoni went into the village to buy rice cakes for her girls, but a tiger stopped her as she walked home. He came out of nowhere—as if he had jumped from the sky—and stood right in front of her, blocking the path.

You have something I want, *the tiger said.*

Now, when a tiger wants something from you, it's very

hard to escape. The best thing to do? Run. Don't talk to the tiger. Definitely don't listen.

So the halmoni tossed him the rice cakes to distract him, and as he swallowed them whole, she ran.

Delicious! *the tiger cried. But if you give a tiger a rice cake, he's going to want something to go with it.* More!

Halmoni didn't get far. The tiger caught up and pounced in front of her. But Halmoni was out of treats, so he gobbled her up, swallowed her whole, like a rice cake. The only thing left was her head scarf, floating gently to the ground.

Still, the tiger wanted more. He wasn't satisfied—tigers never are—but he was clever.

He took Halmoni's head scarf, and when he went to the little cottage days later, he wore it as a disguise.

Knocking on their door, the tiger said, Little girls, I am your halmoni. I am locked out in the rain and cold. Let me in. *He ran his claws against the walls of the house.*

Skritch, skritch, skritch.

The little girls knew something was wrong. Their halmoni's nails were never quite so long, *never so* dirty. *Halmoni liked her manicures.*

But the girls missed their halmoni so much. The tiger said, Little girls, I have rice cakes for you. Little treats for Unya, for Eggi.

The little sister wanted her halmoni so badly. And the tiger called to her, Trust me, Little Egg. Believe.

So she ran to the front door and pulled it open.

Eggi held her breath, waiting. And the tiger roared.

Here's a lesson: never trust a tiger.

Eggi quickly realized the tiger was not her halmoni. (Halmoni was not the roaring type.)

So the girls ran, and the tiger chased them, across deserts and oceans, mountains full of snow and forests thick with rain. They ran and ran until the land just stopped. A deep pit of nothing stretched out in front of them—end of the world, end of the story.

This is it, *Unya cried.*

The tiger closed in on them. He was so hungry.

Help! *Eggi thought. She shut her eyes and begged the sky god.* Save us! Please please please.

To her surprise, the sky god talked back. Hmmm, *he said.* Okay, fine. But tell me a story in exchange.

Not even sky gods can resist a story.

So Eggi and Unya thought fast, and they told him a story.

I don't think you'll be shocked to hear that the sky god saved the girls. Stories like these have happy endings. Just as the tiger leapt to swallow them, a magic rope fell from one end of the sky, and a magic staircase from the other.

Unya grabbed the rope, and Eggi took the stairs, and they climbed—up and up until finally they were safe in the sky kingdom.

There, the sky god told them they could stay with him

forever, but they needed jobs. Living in the sky kingdom? It's expensive.

So the older sister became the sun, and the younger sister became the moon.

Unya was happy, but Eggi cried. Everyone always stared up at the moon, and she didn't like that. She wanted to hide.

So the elder offered to trade places. Don't worry. You can be the sun instead. Nobody can stare at the sun.

Problem solved! They were happy again, and they took their places at opposite ends of the sky, safe forever.

And the tiger? There he was, way back down on earth, asking to come up. But the sky god wouldn't listen. He didn't want to hear a tiger's story, so the tiger was banished.

When I was little, when Halmoni told us this story year after year, I was always satisfied with the ending. I never wondered about the tiger.

I never stopped to ask: What was the tiger's story?

I never stopped to think: What would happen if the tiger came back?

6

I wake up sweating. Sheets twisted, pillow damp, bed creaking. My stomach growls, and I realize I'm desperately hungry for midnight kimchi, so I untangle my blankets and slip out of bed. As I tiptoe across the room, past my sister, I beg the noisy floorboards to keep quiet. They don't listen. They whine under my feet.

Still, Sam doesn't stir.

I walk out of my room and down the stairs, gripping the railing, squinting in the dark, trying to see through the shadows.

Something is weird about the shadows.

They seem to dance and bend in front of me, like they're cast by something I can't see.

I rub my eyes and shake the sleep out of my head, and

the shadows go back to normal. I creep down the stairs, past Halmoni's bedroom, past Mom sleeping on the couch.

I tiptoe toward the kitchen—

And then I stop.

The boxes that were pressed up against the basement door have been shoved aside, leaving a clear path.

I know Mom wanted to move the boxes, but I didn't think she cared enough to upset Halmoni. And anyway, she wanted to move the boxes over to the wall—not just a few inches to the side.

Even weirder: the door's cracked open.

An invisible weight presses against my chest, making it hard to breathe.

Outside, tree branches blow in the wind, *skritch*ing against the windows, and the basement door seems to sway back and forth, just a little.

I creep closer to the door.

Don't get me wrong: I've seen scary movies before. Sam and I used to watch them together, and even though I spent the whole time with my head buried in her shoulder, I know the rules:

1. Don't go into the basement.
2. And definitely don't go *alone.*

But this is different. This isn't one of those scary basements.

Sam and I spent a lot of time playing in this basement whenever Mom was gone. We would act out the stories Halmoni told us and invent fairy tales of our own. With all of Halmoni's old things, there was always something new to discover.

That basement was my favorite place.

And now, it calls out to me. It tugs at my chest, and I feel it somewhere deep inside, right behind my stomach.

The wooden door is warm against my palm, and it creaks when I push it open.

I hold my breath, waiting, not sure if I'm afraid or excited.

Nothing happens.

I fumble for the light switch, which apparently doesn't work, so I go by the moonlight that spills in through a thin window at the top of the wall. The splintering wood prickles against my bare feet as I walk down the steps, and then I'm at the bottom.

First, I'm relieved, because the basement's empty.

Then, I'm upset, because it's empty.

The basement is small, actually. It felt bigger when I was little. The room used to be a puzzle: How do you get from one end to the other? Which boxes do you climb over? What path do you take?

Now: nothing.

Nothing at all, not even water—even though Halmoni said the basement had flooded. I kneel on the floor and run my hand over the carpet. It's bone dry.

Shouldn't it be damp? And shouldn't it smell, I don't know, *wet*? Mildewy?

The basement smells like it always has—dusty and full of memories, like the pages of an old book.

I bite the inside of my cheek. Maybe I'm being paranoid, but none of this makes sense. If the basement never flooded, why would Halmoni move all her things?

And why would she lie?

A noise startles me and I jump to my feet. It's a deep, groaning, animal kind of noise, and I stumble back toward the steps, tripping over my own feet. Fear nips at my toes as I run up the stairs—taking them two at a time, barely bothering to breathe until I'm out of the basement, door shut firmly behind me.

I lean against the shut door and steady my breath and my wobbly legs.

I should go to bed now. That's enough for one night, and I've lost my appetite.

I hear the noise again, and now I realize it's coming from the bathroom. The door hangs ajar and I linger in the dark, peeking in.

And inside the bathroom—I see a shadow beast, a

mess of black scales, hunched over and heaving. It growls and moves like all its bones are broken.

My heart freezes over, but then the shadows slip away—

And it's not a beast at all. It's Halmoni. And something's wrong.

7

I try to process what I'm seeing, but it doesn't make sense. Not a monster at all, but Halmoni.

Halmoni, sick.

Halmoni, throwing up.

Kids get sick all the time. Sam always tells me, *You kids are made of germs.* (As if *she's* such a grown-up). But she's not wrong. Because grown-ups aren't supposed to throw up. And Halmoni, especially, isn't supposed to throw up. Halmoni is so glamorous, and this is so . . . *gross.*

Halmoni has always been the queen of sleep. She goes to bed at eight-thirty, sets her hair in curlers and wraps it in a head scarf, wears a face mask, and sleeps for twelve hours.

Nothing gets in the way of beauty sleep. Except, I guess, this.

A good granddaughter would help her. A good girl would bring her crackers and water and hold her hair.

But for some reason, I don't move. As much as I try, I can't force my legs to work, can't make my hand push the door open.

I am not a good granddaughter.

I feel like I've seen something I shouldn't have. Halmoni looks through the cracked open door and sees me. Too late, I try to switch on my invisibility—but Halmoni sees me. She always does.

"Lily," she croaks. The curlers in her black hair look like scales. "I thought I hear you there."

Her face is draped in darkness, and I can't tell what she's thinking. Is she upset with me? Angry that I'm sneaking around? Does she want me to leave? When I speak, I whisper, "Are you okay?"

She flushes the toilet and stands up, stepping forward, into the moonlight. The wrinkles around her eyes and lips are deeper than usual, but she looks healthy enough. If I hadn't heard her throwing up, I wouldn't have guessed it. "Of course I'm okay. My whole family is here. That's even better than okay."

"But . . ." My voice cracks. I clear my throat. "Are you—are you sick?"

"Oh, yes, Lily. Only a little bit. How do you call it? A little beetle?"

Sometimes I think she mixes up words on purpose, to make us laugh—to distract us. "A bug?" I clarify.

She nods. "Yes, little bug. But I am okay."

I take a breath to calm down. Everybody gets the stomach flu, even halmonis.

Just a little beetle-bug.

"Why you up?" she asks.

"I couldn't sleep. I was thinking about . . . the tiger."

She looks at me for three long heartbeats, then holds out her hand. "Come lie with me," she says. "I tell you now. I tell you what I stole."

8

Halmoni takes me into her bedroom, and I curl up under the covers with her. In the dark, I scan the room.

On her nightstand, as usual: framed photos of me, Mom, Sam.

Also on her nightstand, new: a row of tiny orange pill bottles. A whole family of them.

Before I can ask about them, she says, "I stole stories."

I suck in air, trying to understand, but it's a little hard. My grandmother. Stole stories. From magical tigers.

Not a whole lot of that makes sense.

"How do you steal a story?" I ask.

Halmoni is quiet for so long that I think maybe she's changed her mind about telling me. But she's just waiting, building suspense, and she takes my hand, traces my life line with her fingertip. She used to do this when

I was little, to soothe me during the scary parts of her stories.

"Those stories come from a time before. Long, long ago. When tiger walked like man."

I nudge closer to her, heart humming at those magic words.

"Those stories come from a time when the night is black. Only darkness. And in the darkness, a princess lives in a castle in the sky. The princess very lonely, so she whisper stories to the night. And those stories become stars."

When Halmoni told us to reach up and grab a story from the sky, I always thought it was just a fun game. I never thought she meant it literally. "The stars are made of stories?"

"Yes, yes. Now listen." She shushes me and continues. "The sky princess tell so many stories that the sky fill with light. No more darkness anywhere! And the people on earth, down in villages, they so happy. No more night."

I look out the window at the inky black, and I shiver. *No more night.*

"Story magic was so bright and powerful that of course tigers want it. They go to very top of highest mountain, surround themselves with stars, and guard the sky."

Halmoni continues, "And humans love those stories, too. But I don't like some of the stories stars tell. Some of those stories . . . are dangerous. Some stories too dangerous to tell."

I pause. "But how can a story be dangerous?"

Halmoni wraps her arms tight around me. "Sometime, they make people feel bad and act bad. Some of those stories make me feel sad and small."

I bite my lip. The stories Halmoni told us always had happy endings. They were about clever girls and loving families and warrior princesses who saved the day.

"I hear my halmoni cry when she tell me sad stories, our Korean history," she says. "I see my neighbors get scare. My friends get angry. And I think: Why do we have to hear bad stories? Isn't it better if bad stories just go 'way?"

I swallow. That makes sense, I think.

"So one quiet night, I take jars from my house and carry them up the mountain, tracking those tigers all the way to the caves.

"I am the littlest girl in the littlest village, and I am sneaky. I hide outside the caves and wait until the tigers fall asleep, until their snores echo through the land. And then I get to work, grabbing the stars—the bad stories—in my fists, stuffing them into jars."

It's another thing that seems impossible—but maybe the world is bigger than I thought. Maybe there's room for disappearing tigers and captured stars.

"You stole the stars," I say.

"Not all. But . . . yes."

I wonder what it would feel like to hold stars in my hands—if they would crumble like dust or shatter like glass, if they'd burn fierce and hot or sharp and cold.

Halmoni continues, "I seal jars up. Then I tiptoe away from cave, so soft, *hush-hush.* Before I leave, I think, *I be extra safe. I make sure they don't follow.* So I take rocks from the forest, one by one, and stack them at the mouth of the cave, until they make a wall. Big, heavy wall. Until the tigers trapped inside."

I shudder, imagining the tigers clawing on the other side.

"I think: No more bad stories. No more. I never want to hear them again, so I run away, away from my little village, across the ocean, cross the whole world, to a new place. Where I am safe from sadness." Halmoni's voice starts to fade as she gets sleepier. "I steal the stars, and I lock them away."

"How did you know?" I ask, as I press my warm toes against her cold ones. "How did you know you'd be okay?"

"I don't. But I believe in me. When you believe, that is you being brave. Sometime, believing is the bravest thing of all."

"So everything turned out fine?" Halmoni never talked much about how she came to the United States from Korea, and I never thought to ask.

She is quiet for so long that I think maybe she fell asleep. Then she says, "Nothing last forever, Lily. Tigers break free. The tigers very angry. Now they coming for me."

From the living room, I hear a creak, and I tense—but it's probably just Mom, shifting in her sleep.

Halmoni presses her lips to my head, and her words blur together and she falls into dreams. "They hunting me now. They don't stop hunting."

9

My dreams are filled with tigers. When I wake up the next morning, I lie next to my sleeping halmoni, thinking about her story. Questions thunder through my mind.

What stories did she steal? I'm curious, and part of me wants to hear them, even if they're dangerous.

But I have more important questions, like: Did I really see a tiger? If so, I'm pretty sure it was the one that's hunting Halmoni.

We have to do something about that. We can't just wait. We need a plan to protect ourselves.

There's no chance I'm falling back asleep, so I slide out of bed and pad out of her bedroom into the living room.

The clouds block the sun outside and paint the house

gray, and the living room is so silent that I'm surprised to find Mom sitting on the couch.

She's turned slightly away from me, body curled around a half-full mug of coffee. The steam dances and floats up to kiss her face, but she doesn't notice.

I realize it's been a long time since I've seen Mom so *still*. She's always moving. Right now, I feel like I've captured a precious moment. I want to take it and hold it close to my heart.

She's staring out the living room window, but there's nothing to see except the vague outlines of trees and a few houses in the distance.

I step toward her, and the floorboard yelps.

She flinches. Hot coffee sloshes in her mug, threatening to spill over. "Lily! You scared me. You're so quiet, always sneaking up on me."

"Oh," I say. It's not like I meant to sneak up on her. "Sorry."

She just smiles. "How are you? How did you sleep?"

That's too complicated to answer, so I nod in response.

And I guess a nod is good enough for Mom, because she doesn't push it. She plunks her mug on the coffee table as she stands—and when she does, I notice she's dressed nicely, in a button-down shirt and work pants. "Are you hungry?" she asks.

"No," I say. "What are you wearing?"

"I've got a job interview this morning," she explains, as she clatters around the kitchen.

We've only been here for one night. Most moms would want to settle in and unpack, but of course my mom's already got an interview lined up. She worked as an accountant back in California, and she worked a lot.

"But I have time to make you something," Mom continues. "You really should eat. How about leftover rice cakes?"

"No thanks," I say. "I was actually wondering about—"

"You sure?" she asks. "They're good heated up. Did I ever tell you that Halmoni used to sell her rice cakes when we first moved here? Everyone loved them."

I step forward. "Really?" Mom rarely talks about when she was a kid.

"What about tea? Would you like some tea? I can get you some." Mom opens a cabinet, then stops, hand hovering in the air. "Right. Halmoni moved the mugs to the other side. It was different before." She grabs a mug from its new home and starts making a cup of tea, even though I don't really want one. I don't like tea.

"Mom . . . ," I say, hesitating, trying to sound as casual as possible. "Did Halmoni ever tell you stories when you were little? Stories that seemed impossible?"

Mom frowns. "Oh, I don't know. Maybe. But I was never a big reader like you. I liked to get outside and play, so I didn't really have the patience for stories."

"Oh." I get a feeling that happens sometimes, like something's wrong with me, but I push it aside. "But did she tell you stories about her childhood and stuff?"

Mom's eyes get faraway, like when she was staring out the window. "She never talked about her time in Korea much. I know she grew up poor, in a rural village miles away from Seoul. I know she lived alone with her own halmoni. I know her mom moved to the States when she was very little. Halmoni tried to find her when she moved out here herself—when I was just a baby—but I don't think she ever did."

"I meant more like . . ." Except how do I even explain this? *Did you ever find stars hidden in jars? Did tigers ever chase you?* "Never mind."

Mom takes a breath and plasters a smile on her face. "Anyway, you should meet some kids in the neighborhood. I have some high school friends with kids your age. I can set up a playdate." Mom does this when she wants to change the subject—just abruptly switches topics and acts like we were talking about it the whole time.

I don't bother explaining that "playdates" expired about six years ago. And I don't explain how hard it is to make friends.

Some people, friends just stick to them. Like Sam. Even though she's mean sometimes, she always has a cloud of people around her. She has infinite texts to respond to. But I've never been a sticky person.

I've had a few friends, and a group of girls I hung out with for a while. Sam said they were also QAGs—quiet Asian girls, like me—but eventually they just floated away. They were never mean or anything, but they just forgot to invite me to things. Like they forgot I existed.

They didn't stick.

And I guess that's okay. That's just my invisibility.

"I'm heading to my interview now," Mom says. "But you should get out of the house. Get some fresh air. Maybe go to the library? You might meet some reader kids there. And you love libraries."

I like libraries, I guess. But I don't know where she got the idea that I *love* them, especially when I used to hate the one across the street.

When I was little, I refused to enter it. I'd sit on the steps while Mom and Sam went, and I'd wait for them to bring me picture books.

Mom didn't understand why I was so afraid, because the library looks like a cute cottage, placed right in front of the forest. The door and window frames were painted in bright, colorful patterns.

But I told her: *It looks like the gingerbread house from "Hansel and Gretel."*

I guess she's forgotten about that.

A flash of annoyance flares up in me, but I shove it down. "Yeah, okay."

Mom looks relieved. "That's great, Lily. You're the best. Have I told you you're the best?" She sets the tea in front of me and ruffles my hair. "Have fun at the library, okay?"

She leaves, slamming the front door behind her, and I sip the tea I don't really want. It burns my tongue and tastes like earth, but it sends fire down my throat and wakes me up.

And I'm angry. Because sometimes it's like she has this whole other Lily in her head. An Almost Me that doesn't match the Real Me.

I don't *like* tea. I don't *love* libraries. And what if I'm not the best? How would she know? It's not like she's paying attention.

I get up to pour the tea down the sink, and the swirl of brown water thrills me. It feels reckless and wasteful, but in a good way.

I drop the mug in after it—only with too much force. The mug cracks.

For a moment I stare at the crack, and something opens inside me—something big and gaping, a black hole that's a little too scary to look into.

As quickly as it came, my anger leaks away. I don't

know what got into me. I take the mug and bury it in the trash, all the way at the bottom of the bin, where nobody will find it.

Then I change into jeans and a striped T-shirt, and I braid my hair without bothering to brush it. I pull on my raincoat and head across the street to the library.

I'm not a little girl anymore. I'm not afraid of "Hansel and Gretel." I'm not afraid of fairy tales.

And I don't think I'll find any "reader kids" there, but maybe I'll do some research.

If a tiger is hunting my grandmother, I'll find a way to protect us.

10

The steps leading up to the library are lined with cracks, the windows are tinted, and the roof sags, just a little, like it's tired. It's hard to imagine this is the same gingerbread library I was afraid of as a kid. All that magic has faded.

When I reach the doors, I tug once, then again, and just when I'm wondering whether it's locked, the building finally lets me in. Inside, it smells like mildew, but it's warm.

An older man, sitting at the front desk, looks up from an ancient computer. Thin wire-framed glasses perch on his nose, and a thick white mustache twitches between his pink cheeks. If he weren't frowning so hard, he might look a little like Santa Claus.

"May I help you?" he asks, in a way that says he doesn't

really want to help me. He crosses his arms over his chest, wrinkling his cable-knit sweater.

So, no evil witch, but a grumpy Santa is pretty close.

"Um, that's okay," I tell him. "I'm just looking."

He stares at me, and I'm not sure what to do. For a second, I wonder if I'm not allowed in the library. But that's ridiculous. It's a *library.*

"You have a card?" he asks.

I'm not sure what he means at first. "Oh, right. A library card. Um . . . no."

I step up to the desk, even though he kind of scares me. His bushy eyebrows knit together, and he seems to be waiting for something, but I'm not sure what he needs.

"I'm Lily," I tell him. "Lily Reeves? My hal—my grandma lives across the street. I just moved in with her."

His eyebrow quirks up, and he nods once, in what might be approval. He's still frowning, but less so. "You're Ae-Cha's granddaughter," he confirms. "I'll put your card under her account."

I thank him as he types my information on his clacky keyboard.

"Good woman," he says after a few moments. "Shock to this town's system when she moved here, that's for sure. But I owe her. And Joan—your mother?—followed her everywhere."

"Oh," I say. I'm not sure why he owes her. I'm also not sure about Mom following Halmoni everywhere. I try to picture that, but I can't do it. They're just too different.

He scans a red library card and hands it to me. "Goodbye, then."

"Oh," I repeat, taking the card and slipping it into my pocket. "Um, actually, I'm wondering if you have any books about tigers?"

He frowns, moving to the computer. "Is this a summer school project? Or a personal interest?"

"Personal?" My mouth says it like a question.

He grunts. "Not very often that kids these days use the library. They think you can find everything on the web."

"Yeah," I say, because I'm not sure how else to respond. I'm guessing most Kids These Days don't have a magical tiger that's hunting their grandma, because I don't think Googling *magical evil tiger* would get very good results.

Somebody groans behind me, and I turn to see a girl about Sam's age, with medium-brown skin, freckles, and curly hair, pushing an empty library cart. "Joe, are you really *kids-these-days*-ing this poor girl?"

"I am not wrong," the librarian—Joe—says.

The girl shakes her head at Joe and sticks her hand out to me. "Hello! Welcome to Sunbeam's world-famous library! I'm Jensen."

When I shake her hand, her grip is strong and warm. The splatter of freckles across her cheekbones seems to dance as she smiles. Halmoni always says freckles are lucky.

"This is Jensen," Joe adds, unnecessarily. "She is my employee."

Jensen laughs. "What an eloquent introduction. Now that you know all there is to know about me, what's your name?"

"Lily," I tell her.

She smiles. "Well, Lily, nice to meet you. Have you been here before?"

I shake my head, and her smile grows even wider. "Cool. Honestly, most people in this town probably haven't. We're looking for ways to drum up some life in the place. Remind people we're here and such, but, well, who knows?" She shrugs, then leans over Joe's desk to read his computer screen. "Tigers. Cool. Come with me—I can give you a tour and show you the wildlife section."

Joe returns to his computer, and I follow Jensen through the stacks of books.

"Spoiler alert: the library is pretty sparse, so the tour won't last very long." She laughs. This girl is quick to smile, quicker to laugh.

As we weave through the aisles, I'm reminded of

Halmoni's basement. Before she moved all the boxes and cabinets upstairs, they used to form a maze of memories. I breathe in.

Jensen turns to me. "Are you new in town?"

I tell her I've moved in with Halmoni, and she grins.

"I know your grandma. Everyone loves her."

"Really?"

She tilts her head, looking a bit confused. "Yeah, of course. She's, like, super nice and interesting, and she always wears the best clothes."

I feel a rush of pride, because *of course* everybody loves Halmoni. They *should* love Halmoni.

But at the same time, weirdly, my chest tightens. I don't know anything about Halmoni's life in Sunbeam. Aside from my early years here, I've only known her in California. And in California she was there just for us. She was *ours*.

The jealousy that bubbles up startles me—just like my anger at Mom this morning. I don't like it. These are feelings I shouldn't be feeling.

I refocus on Jensen, who keeps talking. "I tutor for middle school language arts. So if you're ever looking for help, let me know."

My voice scratches when I speak, like it always does when I talk to strangers. "Yeah, okay. Thank you."

The tour ends with a small room in the back of the

library. Inside I see a mini-refrigerator, a cupboard, two chairs, and the back door of the library. On the wall by the door is a faded poster of a cat hanging from a tree, with the words *HANG IN THERE* written in white bubble letters. I don't know who put that up, but I'm pretty sure it wasn't Joe.

"This is the staff room," Jensen explains, "but I always tell my tutees they can come back here. This room is chock-full of sweets, and everyone could use some sugar."

She pulls a chocolate cupcake out of the refrigerator and hands it to me.

Flash-fast, my childhood fear flares up—Hansel and Gretel were lured in by sweets. But I shake away my panic and thank her as I accept the cupcake.

Jensen leans in and lowers her voice. "I'll let you in on a secret: Joe made it."

I raise my eyebrows, and she laughs.

"I know, right?" she says. "He doesn't seem like the baking type. But don't judge him too harshly. He's not so bad once you get to know him. I always say that Joe is, like, a metaphor for this whole town. Kind of a bummer on the outside, but really wonderful when you dig a little deeper."

I get the sense that Jensen is what Mom calls an *unrelenting optimist,* but her happiness is infectious. I smile and take a bite, and the chocolate lights up my whole body. "It's really good," I tell her. For some reason, the cupcake reminds me of Halmoni's rice cakes, even though they don't taste similar at all. "He could sell these."

She gives me an odd look, and I'm instantly embarrassed. I don't know why I said that. Halmoni may have sold her rice cakes, but she did it because she needed money when she moved here.

Jensen grins. "That's a brilliant idea, Lily."

"Oh, okay," I say. I can't tell if she really means it or if she's just being nice.

"Anyway," she continues, "feel free to sneak some whenever you visit. And I hope you do visit. It gets a little lonely around here."

I like Jensen. She's nicer than I thought teenagers could be. She is, basically, the anti-Sam. And I don't know *what,* exactly, she sees when she looks at me, but I know she sees me—which feels nice and also a little itchy.

Jensen leads me over to the wildlife section, and I flip through the tiger selection. It's pretty dismal—*102 Tiger Facts!* and *102 MORE Tiger Facts!*

I skim them, looking for any information to help—something like: *There's a certain breed of tiger that can magically disappear!* Or: *If a tiger is hunting your grandma, here's how to stop it!*

But what I get is:

- A tiger's canine tooth can cut through bone!
- If you look a tiger in the eye, it might be less likely to kill you—but beware!
- The roar of the tiger has such a low frequency that it can paralyze you!

I push the books back onto the shelf. This isn't what I need and it's not making me feel so great about being hunted by a tiger.

"Actually"—I swallow, nervous now—"do you have any stories about tigers?"

Jensen twirls a curl around her finger. "Well, we have the Narnia books. Although, I guess that's a lion. . . . Do you have any stories in mind, in particular? Maybe you can give me a better sense of your tastes."

Obviously, I can't tell her about the magical tiger and the stolen stars, but I can tell her Halmoni's original tiger story.

I give the shortest summary possible. "Well, there's this one story about a tiger and he eats, um, a grandma, and then he dresses up in the grandma's clothes and tries to eat her granddaughters. And then he chases them and—"

"That sounds like 'Little Red Riding Hood'!" Jensen interrupts.

"No, that's a wolf," I say. "And this story is from Korea."

She runs her finger along the book spines, absent-mindedly. "I've never heard the Korean version. Isn't that interesting, though? There are different versions of certain fairy tales from all over the world—even in places that don't overlap. And yet the stories are essentially the same."

I want to explain that this story is completely different. That this is a story about sisters and the sun and the moon and a tiger. It's special.

But Jensen continues, "It's kind of like these folktales have a mind of their own. Like they're floating around the world, waiting for somebody to come along and tell them."

My insides go icy. I imagine that the stories Halmoni stole are alive, locked away somewhere, desperate to escape. "Right," I whisper.

"I doubt we have a book of Korean folktales in this library, though." She raises an eyebrow. "To be honest, this town is pretty white, so you're not going to find much about other cultures. Like, sometimes I pick up waitressing shifts at the only Asian restaurant in town—you know, Dragon Thyme? And I know, it's a pretty cheesy name, and there's no thyme in Asian food, but that's just the town we live in. . . ." She clears her throat. "Anyway, I'll ask Joe to place an order for a book of Korean folktales. Depending on the budget . . ."

I stop listening, because out of the corner of my eye, I catch a flick of a tiger tail—a flash of orange-black, disappearing into the next aisle.

My heart stumbles.

The superpower of invisible girls is to hide, to disappear. To stay out of trouble. That's what I'm good at.

Run away, I tell myself. *Hide.*

But my legs ignore me. I'm already moving down the aisle as I stammer to Jensen, "Actually, I think—uh—there might be a book. Over there!"

I chase the tiger, winding through the aisles, following glimpses of its tail . . . until I slam right into a blur of black and orange.

11

It's not a tiger. It's a boy.

A short white boy, wearing a bright orange shirt, black jeans, and an old-fashioned newsboy hat over shaggy brown hair.

"Sorry!" I blurt. I look over his shoulder. I could have sworn I saw a tiger tail, but there's nothing. We're just standing in one of the aisles, surrounded by comic books.

The boy laughs and tips his hat. "Hello, I'm Ricky. *I'm* sorry we had to meet in a collision situation."

Before I can respond, he shouts to Jensen, who runs up behind me. "Hey, Jensen! You know I *ran* here? From where my dad dropped me off in the parking lot? Because I know you hate when I'm late." He wipes pinpricks of sweat off his upper lip, for dramatic affect. "So it was really considerate of me, just saying."

Jensen sighs. "Ricky, please keep your voice down."

When Ricky grins, the corners of his eyes crinkle, and little dimples form on his round cheeks. I can tell he's one of those sticky people, because I like him right away.

He turns back to me. "So, hello, who are you and what is your story and why are you in this sad little library?"

"I'm Lily," I say, and then my mind goes blank. He stares at me, waiting for more, and I wish my invisibility would kick in right about now.

Jensen saves me. "Lily just moved in with her grandmother, in the house across the street from here."

Gesturing to Ricky, Jensen adds, "Lily, this is Ricky, one of my summer tutees. We meet every Tuesday and Thursday." She turns directly to Ricky and says, "And the library isn't *sad*. It's just a little run-down."

"Is she getting tutored with me?" Ricky asks Jensen, as if I'm not there. I get the same feeling I have with Mom and Sam sometimes—like I'm in the way, or I've walked into a conversation I don't belong in. Or, I guess, ran into it.

I dig my toe into the floor. "No, I'm just looking for books."

His eyes go wide, and he looks at the shelves of comics. "Do you like comics, too? I love them. I'm reading through the original *Supermans* right now. Well, the issues that Joe has here, at least. I know a lot of people think

Superman's not cool. And I'm not saying he's my favorite superhero. He's just canon, you know?"

"Yeah, he's . . ." I pause, trying to think of something to continue the conversation, anything I know about Superman. I draw a blank.

Thankfully, Jensen chimes in. "Lily likes tigers, so she's looking for books about them," Jensen tells him. Which is kind of embarrassing. I want to correct her: I don't *like* tigers. But I shrug and force a smile.

Ricky's grin returns. "Whoa. I've never met a girl who likes tigers before."

"Well . . . yeah." If I were more like Sam, I would tell him that boys don't have dibs on liking tigers. But I don't say anything. I just wish we could go back to talking about comics.

"I mean, not that many girls talk to me, I guess," he continues, unaware of any awkwardness. "But tigers are cool. They're, like, sleek and elegant, but in a ruthless way."

I don't exactly want to think about how ruthless tigers are. "You can't trust a tiger," I say.

He nods slowly. "You can't trust a tiger," he repeats, like I've said something fascinating and he's trying to commit it to memory. "I like that. My great-grandpa was a tiger hunter. But that's actually really bad, because tigers are endangered and that's illegal now, so my dad doesn't want me to tell people about that." He pauses. "I mean . . ."

"Okay, that's enough stalling for now," Jensen says. "Let's get to work, Ricky."

She drags him away, and they leave me standing in the aisle, head whirling.

Maybe I imagined the tiger, but I don't think so. The tiger was here. I *know* it was here.

What would have happened if Ricky hadn't interrupted? What would have happened if I'd caught it?

A sleek, elegant, ruthless, magical tiger is hunting my family, and *I chased it*.

I can't tell if that was incredibly brave or incredibly dangerous. Or maybe a bit of both.

12

The next afternoon, Mom's at another interview, and Halmoni naps through lunch—which is unusual, because even though Halmoni loves to sleep, she loves eating even more.

Sam's upstairs on her computer, and I have nothing to do but snack on peanut butter cups, pace, and think about the tiger.

Here's what I know:

1. The tiger found Halmoni. Or at least, the tiger found *me,* which means it will find Halmoni soon enough.
2. Tigers are determined. It wants the stories, and it will do whatever it takes to get them back. The kosa should have kept

the tiger away, but I saw it in the library, so that obviously didn't work.
3. We need more protection, and even though talking about the tiger upsets Halmoni, I need to tell her.

When I can't pace any longer, I slip into Halmoni's bedroom. The dust dances in the air, catching in the windowlight, and the misty light from outside makes the room hazy. It feels like I've stepped into a separate world, like a little mini universe, trapped in time.

I pull back the covers and gently shake my grandmother awake. "Halmoni," I whisper. "Halmoni, wake up."

She mumbles and turns over in bed, so I shake her again. A little harder. Maybe a little too hard.

She cracks her eyes open. "Lily Bean?" she murmurs. "You hungry?"

"Not really," I say. Honestly, I'm pretty full on peanut butter cups.

She climbs out of bed—slowly and intently, like she's climbing out of quicksand. Sitting on the edge of the mattress, she stretches, and I can almost see the sleep sliding off her.

She looks weak.

"Halmoni," I blurt, my tiger questions temporarily on hold, "is the bug gone? Are you sure you're okay?"

"I am better than okay. My family is here. That is all I ever want." She smiles, but her words wobble. "You stop worry."

"Speaking of worrying . . ." I tug at one of my braids. "I think we need more protection than just kosa. I saw the tiger again."

For a second, fear ignites in Halmoni's eyes. But then she closes them and shakes her head. When her eyes open again, she is soft and smiling.

She opens her nightstand drawer and pulls out a sheaf of dried herbs. Then she breaks off a piece and places it in my palm. "This for you. This make you safe, okay? So you don't worry anymore."

I stare at the shriveled plant and look up at her. "What is it?"

"This mugwort," she explains. "This my medicine to eat, but you don't eat. You keep in you pockets, and it give you protection."

I thank her and slip the dried herb into my pocket.

"And this . . ." She hesitates before reaching behind her neck and unlatching the necklace. The silver chain with the pearl pendant—her special necklace, the one she wears every day, the one she rubs between her fingers when she's trying to find the right English words. "This help, too. You wear for protection, and it keep you safe."

My pulse beats in every limb as she fastens it around my neck. It's heavier than it looks. "But this is yours," I say.

"Yes, and now it is yours."

I press my palm against the pendant. It's warmer than I expected. It warms my chest, and I like the way it feels, heavy above my heart. "Did this really keep you safe?"

"I am here, yes?"

I pinch the pearl between my fingers, and it seems to buzz with energy. "But what about you? Don't you still need protection? The tigers are hunting."

She smiles, but it's not a regular Halmoni smile. It doesn't match her eyes. "I be safe, Lily. I am not worrying."

I'm not so sure, and when she sees that in my eyes, she says, "Okay, we go grocery now. We get even *more* protection, extra help against bad spirits. We buy pine nuts to burn and rice to scatter under full moon. Also, I need fresh ingredient for rice cake."

I smile, feeling better.

She leans closer. "And I buy you favorite treats, because I am best." She pauses. "Well, you mother is best. But . . . I am *best* best."

I laugh. "You are."

She raises an eyebrow. "Now go tell Sam."

After I call Sam downstairs and tell her where we're

going, she leans on the dining table, crossing her arms. "That's not a good idea. Didn't Mom say you're not supposed to drive?"

Halmoni's eyes dart away, and I get the urge to pinch my sister. Sam is a black hole for happiness.

"*You* can drive if you want," I tell Sam.

She recoils. "I don't know. . . ." She *could* drive. She has her permit, and Halmoni's a licensed driver. Mom keeps bugging Sam to practice.

But, of course, she won't. Sam tried two lessons with her driving instructor and refused to get behind the wheel after that. Nothing bad happened, but she won't do it because of Dad's car accident.

Halmoni presses her palm against Sam's cheek. "Life is not for waiting. We go now. We be okay."

Sam tugs at her white streak. "But Mom said—"

Halmoni tsks. "You mother don't know what she says. I be fine."

Sam looks unsure, which is ridiculous, because Sam never cares what Mom says.

"You can stay here," I tell her.

There's a flash of hurt in her eyes, and then annoyance. "No. I'll come," she says.

Halmoni claps. "Good girls! I go change into fancy clothes."

Sam frowns. "Why?"

"Grocery," Halmoni answers before disappearing into her room.

Sam shakes her head, but a tiny smiles tugs at her lips. And I feel happy, too. Halmoni is Halmoni. Weird is her normal. And I don't have to worry. With one hand, I pat the mugwort in my pocket. With the other, I grasp my pendant. Everything will be okay. I just know it.

We arrive at the grocery store with a short list:

For eating:

- mochi flour, for rice cakes
- wasabi peas, for Mom
- Happy Nut crackers, for Sam
- peanut butter cups, for Lily

For extra protection:

- five-grain rice, to scatter in the woods
- pine nuts, to burn under a full moon

For misc.:

- laundry detergent

Sam raises an eyebrow when she sees the protection category, but she doesn't say anything.

"We have to leave here in half hour, because rain coming soon," Halmoni says.

Sam frowns. "It's not gonna rain today. The weather app says there's a zero percent chance."

Halmoni just pats Sam's head. "Half hour."

"That's fine," I say. "We won't take that long."

I'm about to head off to check the grains aisle, when a woman with bright red curly hair runs right up to us.

"You must be the granddaughters!" she squeals. I'm a little worried she's about to pinch our cheeks, but she refrains.

Halmoni beams. "These my little ones."

"Your grandmother is the greatest," the woman gushes to Sam and me. "She cured my asthma with her plants."

Sam takes a very small step back. "That's cool."

The woman stays to chat with Halmoni for a while, and when she finally flits away, a bald man tells us that Halmoni made him laugh, even after his divorce. And then an older woman tells us that she plays cards with Halmoni.

It's a lot to take in, especially when I'm on a protection-finding mission.

Halmoni introduces Sam and me to everybody she sees, and they all tell us how pretty we are, how sweet. I try to keep track of everyone, but their names slip through my mind, their faces blur together.

Halmoni is so popular here. Everybody knows her. Everybody loves her. And I have no idea who these people are.

After about twenty minutes, Sam pulls me into the cereal aisle to hide.

"Halmoni tricked us," she says. "This isn't a quick grocery run. This is a whole *event.*"

"She knows everyone," I say.

"Yeah, which explains the nice clothes, I guess." Sam grins.

"Halmoni has a lot of friends," I say, checking our list. I guess there's no harm in waiting for Halmoni.

Sam plops down on the floor. "There are so many people we don't know. And they all have a story about her. It's like she has a secret life."

I join her, sitting on the tiles and leaning against the store-brand frosted flakes. I don't say anything, but she knows I agree. Our sister telepathy hasn't disappeared completely.

I pick at the stitching of my jeans. "Speaking of stories . . ." I wait for Sam to roll her eyes, but she doesn't, so I continue. "Halmoni told me this weird one I'd never heard. About tigers."

Sam raises an eyebrow, a silent *Go on.*

I take a deep breath. "You know how Halmoni always said that the stars were made of stories? Well, apparently that's true. And the tigers used to guard them. But Halmoni *stole* some of the stars and hid them in jars or something. And now the tigers are mad."

Sam frowns. "That's a weird story, Lily. Halmoni's crazy."

"She's not crazy. Don't say that. But anyway, she said—"

"When did she tell you all this?"

"The first night we were here, but—"

Her eyes fall to the pendant around my neck. "And when did she give you *that*?"

Automatically, my hand flies to my chest, covering it—as if it's something to hide. "Just now, before we left. She was talking about different kinds of protection."

Sam unties and then reties her shoelaces for no apparent reason. "I don't know why she never talks to me about this stuff."

I didn't realize that Sam *wanted* Halmoni to tell her stuff.

For a second, I consider telling Sam everything—about how I saw a tiger that should be impossible. And about how I *chased* that tiger, even though I knew it was dangerous—and I still can't really explain why.

But then I hear a familiar voice in the next aisle. "Maybe we could make muffins or cupcakes or something? Like we could use Mom's recipe. Or the sticky buns she used to make?"

It's Ricky.

When I rise to my feet and press my ear against the cereal boxes, Sam gives me a look that says, *What is wrong with you?*

I don't have any answer to that. I know it's wrong to eavesdrop, but for some reason, I don't stop myself.

Maybe it's because Ricky is sticky. Or maybe it's just because I'm nosy. Or maybe it's because Ricky was there when I saw the tiger.

I tiptoe down the aisle until I reach the end. There's a big *BUY TWO, GET ONE FREE!* display of Lucky Charms—about a hundred stacked cereal boxes—and I use it as a spy shield. I peek out around the side.

Invisible, I tell myself, calling on my superpower with all my might.

Ricky walks down the aisle with a man who I'm guessing is his dad, because he looks like a grown-up version of Ricky—same messy brown hair, same big blue eyes. I wonder if Ricky's great-grandfather looked like that, too. The tiger hunter.

Sam frowns in confusion and follows me to the end of the aisle. "Lily?" she asks, but I shush her, and she joins me in spying.

"Who's that?" she whispers.

I shake my head so she'll be quiet, but she nudges me in the ribs. Sam is incapable of being invisible.

"I met him at the library," I say, as quietly as I can.

Sam makes a *hmm* noise, a noise that says she knows something I don't know, which is annoying, but I ignore her. I'm busy eavesdropping.

"Connor *loves* that recipe," Ricky's saying. He's looking up at his dad with a kind of desperation, but his dad's not paying attention. "Did I tell you about that one time when I made it, he ate like *four whole servings*? No, not like four. Like six, actually. Then he got really sick and he threw up everywhere and—"

"Ricky, quiet." Ricky's dad massages his temples.

I get this sinking, glued-to-the-ground feeling. This is an awkward family moment. I should mind my own business.

"We probably shouldn't . . . ," Sam murmurs, but I keep watching.

Ricky's dad pushes a cart, scanning the canned goods, and Ricky jogs along after him. "But, Dad, I'm pretty sure I told you this story. Do you remember? It was when we were at the laser tag place, and—"

"Ricky," his dad snaps, so loudly that Sam and I both step back from the cereal.

Ricky looks up at him, face open and hopeful, like he

can't tell his dad is upset with him. "And I shot him right in the chest. With the laser only, so it's not like he could actually feel it, and then—"

"Will you just *shut up*?"

The words echo through me. I feel the horribleness of them in my chest, squeezing hard.

Sam tugs at my shirtsleeve. "Come on," she whispers.

I look over her shoulder to see Halmoni standing at the end of the aisle, basket full, waving us over. She points to her watch and mimes marching and then rain. The grocery store has mostly cleared out by now, and she's worried about the weather.

Gaja, Halmoni mouths. *Let's go.*

But I can't leave now. Staying feels wrong, but leaving feels even worse. I inch closer, pressing myself against the Lucky Charms.

I watch Ricky stop walking, lips frozen midsmile but eyes wide with hurt. Slowly, his smile fades, and he stares down at his shoes.

I lean forward. I don't know this kid, but I know that feeling. I want to reach out and say, *I see you.*

I want to—

Only there's no more time for wanting, because suddenly I'm falling forward.

The cardboard display falls over, and then I'm on top of it, sprawled out on the floor in front of Ricky and his dad and the rest of the grocery store—surrounded by cereal boxes.

"Oh, *man,*" Sam says, backing away from me, as if embarrassment is contagious.

Down the aisle, Halmoni hurries toward me, but her hurrying isn't very fast, and I'm just lying here on the floor.

I look up at Ricky and his dad, who look down at me, staring in surprise.

Ricky blinks. "I know you."

"Um," I say. I try to manage a shrug that says something like *Oh, hi, what a coincidence running into you here!* but is probably more like *I was spying and heard your dad say shut up and now I'm lying on a mountain of cereal.*

"Are you okay?" Ricky's dad asks, looking both startled and concerned.

I nod. "Yeah, totally fine. I was just . . . trying to decide if I wanted cereal. But . . . I don't think . . . I'm going to . . . get it?"

Ricky's smile comes back, spreading slowly across his face. And it's just a *What is she even doing?* smile, but still.

Sam snorts. Which is rude.

I stand up and clear my throat. "Bye!"

I'm very much ready to run away now, but Halmoni's finally made it here, and she stops me.

Halmoni runs a hand over my hair—which is probably a mess—and beams at Ricky and his dad. "Hello, boys!"

Ricky's dad clears his throat. "Hello, Ae-Cha."

Halmoni smiles at Ricky's dad and points at the cereal. "You help me fix that, please?"

He lurches forward and props the cardboard shelf up. It falls right back over. I guess completely crushing it ruined its ability to . . . be a shelf.

"Sorry," I mumble.

"All okay," Halmoni says. "We stack."

So Halmoni, Sam, Ricky, his dad, and I work together, stacking the boxes. It's incredibly uncomfortable. I want to disappear, because they don't *know* that I was eavesdropping—but it's obvious, right?

When we're done, Halmoni puts her hand on the dad's shoulder. "Thank you," she says. "It is always good to help each other when we need it."

She turns to Ricky. "See, I have struggle here, and you dad help me. Sometimes parents and grandparents need help, too."

Sam and I exchange a glance. Now is not the time for one of Halmoni's life lessons.

Turning back to his dad, Halmoni says, "And when Ricky have struggle, you help him. We always remember to help each other. You both good boys, and you have hard times. I know that. But when you have hard times, you come together, not apart. Okay?"

Halmoni glows with both fierceness and kindness. It's like she's lit up from the inside, like she has stars burning inside her.

And I realize: she knows. She must. I'm not sure how she managed to overhear their conversation, but somehow she did.

Ricky and his dad both nod, and the dad looks a little embarrassed. I think he knows he was wrong. Ricky looks over at me, and I shrug, as if I have no idea what Halmoni's doing.

But really, I get it. I wanted to tell Ricky, *I see you,* but Halmoni's talking to Ricky's dad. She's telling him, *I see you, and I see the way you* could *be.*

Even though Halmoni's fierceness had nothing to do with our tiger-protection plan, I can't help thinking I was supposed to see this. This is part of her story.

13

Sam waits until we're in the car, driving back home, and then she bursts out laughing. "I can't believe you *fell over* like that. That was awesome."

"Thanks," I say with sarcasm I learned from her.

She laughs some more, and I shake my head, but now that it's over, it doesn't seem quite so bad.

"And then *Halmoni,*" Sam continues, turning to Halmoni, who's hunched over and squinting at the road ahead. She was right. It did start raining, and because of my cereal disaster, we're caught in it. I feel a little bad, because I know Halmoni didn't want to drive in the rain. But it's okay. We're not too far from home.

"I can't believe you made those guys help, and then you lectured them like that!" Sam says.

Halmoni nods. "When something wrong happen, you fix it."

I can't tell if the wrong thing was me knocking over cereal, or what Ricky's dad said, or maybe both.

Sam shrugs. "Okay, but honestly, that man was a jerk. You were way nicer than he deserved."

Halmoni glances over at Sam, then at me, her eyes serious. "When I very little, before my mom leave, she tell me something important. She say, Ae-Cha, learn this: Everybody have good and bad in them. But sometimes they so focused on sad, scary stories in life that they forget the good. When that happen, you don't tell them they are bad. That only make it worse. You remind them of the good."

I turn her words over in my head. "Is that why sad stories are dangerous, Halmoni? Because they make people bad?"

She starts to answer, but a cough steals her words, and she shudders.

Maybe it's just the shadows of raindrops hitting the windshield and the fading evening light—but I notice that she looks pale. Her skin is splotchy.

She shudders again, and Sam glances back and forth between Halmoni and the road, Halmoni, road. "Halmoni?" Sam asks. She puts her hand on Halmoni's shoulder and is about to say something, when the car shudders, too. Sam grips her armrest. "What's wrong? Halmoni? Are you okay?"

Halmoni doesn't answer. She stares straight ahead, shaking her head slightly.

I follow her gaze—and I see the tiger.

It stands right in front of us, eyes locked on Halmoni's. And the weirdest thing—it's like it's not raining around the tiger. The tiger isn't getting wet, as if there's a protective bubble around it, where the rain refuses to fall.

I turn to Halmoni, and I can tell she sees it, too.

"Not yet," she mutters, eyes straight ahead. "Not ready yet."

Heart racing, I stuff my hand into my pocket, feeling for the mugwort.

Halmoni swerves suddenly. The wheels skid through the rain, and my seat belt slices into my shoulder. The car dives to the side of the road, and Sam screams, and I think I do, too. When we come to a stop—panting, gasping—I can't even see straight.

"Halmoni?" Sam asks again, but Halmoni starts coughing uncontrollably. In the rearview mirror, Halmoni's whole face puckers like a sour plum seed.

Then Halmoni's in motion, and we can't stop her. She opens her door and hobbles over to the side of the road, clutching her stomach, hunched. She drops to her knees, and her body shakes as she coughs.

Sam and I rush out of the car, and I spin around, looking for the tiger, but it's gone.

Halmoni throws up into the grass, and I wrap my arms around my chest.

This is more than a bug.

I stand on the side of the road, in the rain, paralyzed as I watch her. When something wrong happens, we're supposed to fix it—but what if there's nothing we can do?

When Sam turns to me, her face is moon white and her eyes are wide. "What do we do?" she asks—which isn't fair because she's supposed to know. Big sisters are not supposed to get scared. Little sisters get scared, and then big sisters comfort them and say, *It's okay, I'll be the moon.*

"Seriously, what do we *do*?" she repeats, as if by saying it louder she can demand an answer from the universe.

Halmoni heaves, a sound raw and heavy, and I try not to hear it.

"We should call 911?" I say, only it comes out as a question.

Sam shakes her head. "You don't call 911 for vomit." But she doesn't sound so sure. She holds her phone in her hand, staring at it, like she wants it to make the decision for her.

"Do something," I whisper. And Sam stares back, eyes wide, hand shaking.

"Mom," Halmoni gasps. "Call you mom."

Sam dials, and ten minutes later, Mom's tires screech against the road behind us. She throws her car into park behind Halmoni's—and we are saved from having to save our halmoni.

Mom's still in her interview clothes, still in work mode, and she shouts at us as she runs over to help Halmoni up. "What's going on? What are you doing out here? She's not supposed to drive! Why didn't you call me sooner? Sam, I told you to call me if anything went wrong!"

Only she's not really talking to us, because she's busy with Halmoni. She dabs Halmoni's lips with a tissue, rubs her back.

She used to do that to Sam and me when we got sick.

Only we're the kids. And Halmoni is her mom. So everything is upside down.

Mom pulls a pill out of her purse and tries to slip it into Halmoni's mouth. Halmoni turns away, protesting, but Mom insists.

I turn to Sam, looking for answers, but Sam doesn't see me. She's too busy staring at Halmoni, chewing her thumbnail so hard I'm afraid it might bleed.

"I need to take Halmoni to the hospital," Mom says. "Sam, can you drive Lily back?"

Sam's frozen. She can't even answer.

Mom swears. "Fine. Fine. I'll drop you at home first.

We're close enough. All of you, into the car. We're going now."

Sam and I get into the back seat of Mom's car without question, and Mom lifts Halmoni into the passenger side.

"Is Halmoni okay?" I ask.

Mom doesn't answer, so I stare out the window. Above us, the first few stars peek out of the evening sky, and I ask them a silent question: *What do I do?*

The stars seem to dance as we drive past, and even though they are light-lifetimes away, I can almost hear them, singing their stories.

What do I do? I ask again.

They wink at me. *Fix it.*

14

I wake up in the middle of the night. Sam's still sleeping. She was up later than me, waiting for Mom and Halmoni. I don't know if they came home.

And I can't stand not knowing. I can't stand feeling helpless—like I have to fix it, but I don't know how.

Quietly I walk downstairs. Mom's sleeping on the couch, and I crack Halmoni's door open. Inside, she's wrapped in a cocoon of silk sheets, and I feel dizzy with relief. Halmoni's okay. I press my hand against the wall to keep from tipping over. I want to go to her, but the image of her in the road burns in my brain. Leftover fear sits in my chest.

For now, it's enough just to know she's all right. So I shut the door.

As I do, the house groans, shattering the silent night. Shadows dance around me.

And from behind me, someone says, "Hello, Lily." It's a gravelly female voice. It scrapes against my ears like claws on rice paper. "I've been searching for your family for a long, long time."

I spin around, trying to find the source of the voice.

But there's nobody else in the room except for Mom, who's still sleeping.

My rabbit heart panics, pounding against my ribs like it wants to escape.

"Oh, come on now. I'm not that scary." The voice seems to come from all around me—from inside me, even. It echoes in my chest.

The shadows in the kitchen start to take shape, shifting and stretching. And then they come together, forming one shape. The giant shadow steps forward, into the starlight, and it becomes the tiger—big as a car, filling the whole hallway.

"You talk," I whisper. And then, without meaning to, I add, "And you're a girl."

I clamp my lips shut, because what a ridiculous thing to say.

She scoffs. "Typical. You hear one story about a male tiger and think we're all the same? Humans are the worst."

She takes a step toward me and I press myself back. My shoulder blades dig into Halmoni's door.

Maybe I'm trapped in an elaborate dream—but I don't think so. I feel the chill in the air, the brush of goose bumps on my arm, the warped wood beneath my feet, and the pinch in my shoulders as I press them back.

Dreams are not made of details. Are nightmares?

I glance over at Mom on the couch, but she just snores.

"Don't worry," the tiger says. "Your mother won't be bothering us."

My whole body clenches, but the tiger rolls her eyes. "She's a heavy sleeper."

A not-small part of my brain is screaming, *You are talking to a tiger! A tiger is talking to you. This is for-sure impossible.*

I feel a little dizzy. "Go away," I tell her.

The tiger steps closer, tail swishing back and forth. She tilts her head and flicks an ear. "Why so hostile, Little Egg? I am not going to eat you, just so you know. I'm on a kimchi diet."

I stare at her. This is the monster Halmoni warned me about.

She makes a sound that's halfway between a purr and a growl. "Your halmoni stole the stars, and I am here to collect them. That is all. Will you help me, little one?"

My mouth is so dry, I can barely form the word, but I manage. "No."

She sighs. "You humans understand so little of the world, and your halmoni can't see what she's done. She doesn't see what's harming her. I only want to help her. Trust me."

I shake my head, because Halmoni told me not to trust tigers. And it's pretty clear that the tiger is harming her. The tiger was in the road when Halmoni got sick. The tiger scared her.

But the big cat continues, "Story magic is powerful, powerful enough to change someone. And when a story is locked away, its magic only grows. Sometimes it grows sour. The magic becomes a kind of poison. Do you understand?"

I refuse to respond. I won't let her twist lies around my heart.

"Lily Bean, if you return those stories to me, your halmoni will feel better. If they stay locked away, they will make her sick. They will"—her teeth flash—"eat her up."

"You're lying," I say, but my voice cracks.

"I'm offering a deal. You help me find the stories, I'll return them to their place in the sky, and you never have to think about them again. I get my stars back, and we help your halmoni. You don't even have to hear the stories. Everybody wins." The tiger shifts her weight, paw to paw, and her fur glistens in the starlight. "Don't you want to be a hero?"

Here's the scariest part: something deep inside me says yes. I am never the hero—not like Halmoni—and part of me wants to be.

I bite my lip so my yes won't escape.

"You should know"—her voice is so deep it vibrates through me—"this is your one chance to help your halmoni. I won't offer again."

Halmoni told me to be careful, and just the thought of making a deal with the tiger rips my stomach to shreds. But there's so much Halmoni didn't tell me. There's so much she's kept hidden—so much I want to know.

What if the tiger's right? What if these stolen star stories are making Halmoni sick?

I am frozen, trapped in my own thoughts. This is my problem. This is why Sam calls me a QAG. I'm so afraid of saying the wrong answer that I don't say anything at all.

For a few stretched-out moments, the tiger waits. Then she shakes her head. Already she's fading into shadow. "I was hoping you'd surprise me."

I think of Halmoni tonight, and how helpless I felt, and how I need to fix this. "Wait!" I call out. "I'll do it!"

But I'm too late. Her stripes blur into blackness, and she's gone.

15

Obviously, I don't sleep after that. I sit up in bed, chewing my nails, staring out the window until the sun comes up, until I hear a strange noise downstairs—like a whispering through the walls.

The sound persists, and I lean forward, ears straining. This house is full of noises. I tiptoe down the stairs. It could be the tiger, and if it is, I have to accept her offer. Even though I'm still not sure, even though I'm afraid.

But there's no tiger.

When I reach the bottom, it's only Mom and Halmoni, sitting in Halmoni's bedroom with the door cracked just-barely, talking so quietly that their words are a slush of wisps and hisses.

Mom says, "Nobody's offered yet. I'm still looking. But it'll happen soon. I'm hopeful."

"You getting job will be good," Halmoni says. "That is good for you."

"Good for *us,* you mean," Mom says.

"Good for you and the girls."

"Don't do that," Mom says. Her voice cracks, and I can barely hear her. "We have time. I can buy more time."

"No, no. You don't worry about that," Halmoni says. There's that scolding tone in her voice, the one she always gets when she talks to Mom. But there's something else, too. Something softer. "And don't make that worry face. You going to get wrinkles."

"Mom—"

"You wearing sunscreen? Sunscreen help with wrinkle."

"Mom—"

"What about hat? Hat help, too."

"Mom! I don't need a hat. I need *you.*" Mom's voice breaks. When she speaks again, her voice is quiet. "Please just try the other treatments. Don't give up."

Treatments. Hospitals. Buying more time.

An understanding settles in my gut—one I can't quite put into words.

The softness in Halmoni's words evaporates. "You think I just give up? No! I don't want to go. I don't want to leave you. I am not ready. But I don't get to decide. The only thing I decide is how I be *right now.* So you don't take that away from me."

I've never heard Halmoni sound so angry. She is strong and fierce and kind. But now she's different. There's a scary side of her, like there's a tiger hiding just below her skin, straining to get out.

I hear another strange sound, and it's so out of place that I don't recognize it at first. Until I realize: Mom's *crying.*

But Mom never cries.

"Joanie," Halmoni says quietly. "You be strong, for girls' sake."

My stomach twists. I shouldn't be hearing this. I don't *want* to hear this.

"I can't do this," Mom whispers. "Not again. Not after Andy. I can't be strong *again.*"

"I know you can," Halmoni says, "because you are my daughter."

I take a few steps back up the stairs, cloaking myself in the shadows. Halmoni's illness must be really serious, if Mom's crying.

I wish now that it really was the tiger downstairs. Because the truth is, this is scarier than any tiger.

When Mom eventually comes out of the bedroom, I automatically call on my invisibility. But then I change my mind. I don't want to be alone.

I shift my weight, and when stairs creak beneath me, Mom looks up.

"Oh," she says when she sees me. *"Oh."*

Very quietly I ask, "Is Halmoni okay? Are *you* okay?"

Mom's eyes are still red. "Did you hear us talking?"

When I don't answer, she opens her arms and I run down the steps. She crushes me into a hug, and as she takes a breath, I feel the shudder in her lungs. "She's going to be. Don't worry. Everything's going to be fine." Then she straightens up, pulls herself back together. "Would you like some tea? Some breakfast? I'll make you whatever you want."

"I want to know what's going on." I try to sound strong, but my voice is very small.

Mom fiddles with her glasses. "Halmoni's sick, Lily. But we're still hopeful, okay? I'm looking for a new job, so that should bring in money for special treatments. And even if we don't do those treatments, we'll—we can keep her comfortable."

"What kind of sick?" I ask, even though I already know it's the *bad* kind.

Mom grimaces, then pulls me over to the couch. I thunk down next to her, sinking into the cushions.

For once, it isn't raining. Happy sunlight spills through the windows, like the weather is mocking me.

Mom says, "Halmoni has brain cancer."

For a few seconds, my insides go ice-numb. I can't feel anything except for cold and a strange tingling.

"Lily, did you hear me?"

I keep very still, as if I can hide from the pain. As if the truth is a tiger, and if I don't move, maybe it won't find me.

"Honey?"

Except I guess I can't hide for long, because that strange tingling turns jagged, like broken glass. I nod my aching head. I try to say it out loud—*brain cancer*—but I can't.

Mom continues. "That's what's causing the symptoms you might have seen: the nausea, the paranoia, and all the—Well, sometimes with this type of illness, patients can have, uh, hallucinations."

"Hallucinations?"

"This is a lot. I understand. I want you to know that I'm here for you."

"What kind of hallucinations?"

"Oh, Lily." Her eyes soften and she grabs my hands. "It's nothing too scary. Just the little things. Confusing dreams with reality. Like how she thinks the basement flooded—things like that."

So that explains why the basement was so dry. But the other stuff—I saw the tiger, too. I know that was real.

"What if there's a way to help?" I ask.

"Oh, Lily. Let me handle this. And you don't worry. You just spend time enjoying your halmoni and keeping her company. That's why we moved here. So you girls can enjoy her."

Mom squeezes my hands. "I talked to Sam about this last night, when you were asleep, so you can discuss it with her, if that helps. This isn't going to be a onetime conversation. It's an ongoing dialogue, and I'm here any-time, to answer any questions you have."

Questions claw up my throat, but I don't think Mom has the answers. Halmoni said it herself: Mom doesn't believe in stories. Her world is small.

But I know there's a way to help—something that Mom won't, or can't, see.

The tiger can cure Halmoni.

I wasn't brave enough, before, to trust her magic. But this time, I will be.

This time, I'll be ready. The tiger said she wouldn't come to me again, so I'll have to go to her.

Lucky for me, I happen to know a family of tiger hunters.

16

Hyped up on New Plan energy, I run upstairs to tell Sam. Barely awake, she's sitting up in bed with her laptop perched on her knees, wrapped in the glow of her screen.

I rush over to her and push her laptop closed, snapping it shut like the jaws of a tiger.

She pulls her fingers back and stares at me, eyes wide, but before she can get mad, I say, "Sam, there might be a way to make Halmoni better. In the story she told me—"

"No," Sam interrupts. The word thumps against my chest, heavy and cold. "Not right now, please. I'm just not in the mood for stories right now. Stories want you to believe that magic is real and—it's just not."

"Actually . . ." I'm afraid of what she'll say when I tell

her, but I don't want to hold this secret by myself. "I'm not sure it's just a story."

She sighs. "Lily, what are you talking about?"

"I think . . . a tiger, like from the story . . . actually came to me. And talked to me. And the same tiger was in the road yesterday, when Halmoni . . . you know."

She's silent for so long that I think maybe she saw the tiger, too. Maybe she thought she was the only one, and now she's relieved.

But then she says, "You need to get it together. This is some kind of mental stress reaction, or something, because what you're saying is impossible."

"Things are only impossible if you *believe* they're impossible. The tiger—"

"Lily!" she snaps, tugging at the white streak in her hair. "Just stop with this tiger stuff, okay? There's actual real-life stuff going on right now. Don't make it worse."

Where is the Sam from the grocery store? The sister who wanted to hear the stories?

I should have known that wouldn't last long.

"Yeah, you're right," I lie. "I probably imagined it. I'll see you later."

I turn away from her as I change out of my pajamas and into jeans and a sweatshirt. I can find Ricky. I can learn how to hunt a tiger. And I don't need Sam's help.

"Um," Sam says. "Where are you going?"

"Nowhere."

"Wait—" Sam says, but I pretend not to hear her and I thunder back down the stairs. I tell Mom I'm going out, that I don't want to talk anymore. She tries to stop me, but I don't listen.

I run until I reach the heavy library doors, and then I take a few deep breaths, steadying myself.

I have to do this. Halmoni needs me.

I grab the big handle, yank the door open, and slip inside.

Joe's sitting at his desk, and I assume he doesn't want to talk, but he stops me as I pass. "Lily." He clears his throat, halfway between a grunt and a grumble. "I just want to say, you had a good idea."

"Oh," I say, breathless. I have no idea what he's talking about. For a second, I think he discovered my tiger plan, but of course that's impossible.

His mustache twitches. "Jensen said you suggested a bake sale. Not sure how much money that would actually raise, but it does seem like a good way to get the community engaged."

"Oh," I repeat. When I suggested selling the cupcakes, I didn't realize Jensen had taken me seriously. "That's good."

He nods in a way that says, *This conversation is over.*

"Are Ricky and Jensen here today?" I ask.

He gestures to the back of the library, and I make my way through the stacks until I come to a cluster of tables. Ricky and Jensen are sitting together, with an open notebook, a pile of flash cards, and an empty pudding cup between them.

Ricky looks up and grins. Today he's wearing a beanie that says *BEANS*, pulled down to his eyebrows. And if he feels awkward after the grocery-store incident, he doesn't show it.

Maybe that's his superpower—the unpleasant, uncomfortable things don't bother him.

"Lizzie!" he shouts.

It takes me a second to realize he's talking to me, and Jensen smiles apologetically. "It's Lily," she corrects. "Hi, Lily, how are you?"

"Um, good." My words come out a little shaky. I'm nervous now, because what I'm about to ask makes no sense. It's impossible. And I'm going to ask anyway.

Before I can, Jensen says, "I've been meaning to tell you about the bake sale! I didn't want you to think I stole your idea and didn't give you credit for it."

"Oh, I don't—"

"But you can help make flyers and set up and stuff!" She smiles wide, all her freckles lighting up.

"I'm helping, too," Ricky says. Then, in a dramatic whisper, he adds, "We'll get free cupcakes!"

"Uh, yeah, sounds good," I say.

"Cool!" Jensen says. "Now, Ricky and I have to get back to tutoring, so—"

Ricky shoves his notebook aside and leans forward. "So, Lily, sit down. Tell us your whole life story. When did you discover a love of tigers? How do you *really* feel about Lucky Charms? Spare no details!"

"Well . . . ," I start. He mentioned tigers. There's an opening there, somehow. If I can just shift the subject—

"Ricky, stop," Jensen says. And then, to me: "Ignore him. He's just trying to get out of the tutoring session."

Ricky's eyes bug. "No, Jensen, I'm serious! I'm making a friend. Adam is at camp, and Connor is traveling around Italy, and I *must* be socialized."

Jensen snort-laughs. "You *must* review these flash cards."

I'm about to get dismissed, so I interrupt with the first thing that comes to mind. "Jensen, can I have a pudding, too?"

She blinks. It's rude, I know, but I need a second alone with Ricky.

Jensen covers her surprise with a smile and stands up. "Sure, Lily. I'll grab you one. Ricky's desperate for a *quick* break anyway." She raises her eyebrows at Ricky to emphasize *quick,* then asks if I want chocolate or vanilla.

"Vanilla. Thank you." I want to hug her hard, but that seems a little over the top for pudding.

"Another chocolate for me, please," Ricky says.

Jensen sighs and heads off to the staff room.

"The tutoring isn't because I'm stupid," Ricky says as soon as Jensen leaves. "It's just because I don't have a word brain. That's why. Or a numbers one, I guess. But I'm going to be a psychologist. I have a very *intuitive understanding of the human psyche,*" he says, as if he's reciting something he read online. "I'm very good at reading people."

"Oh," I say. "Okay." I have to get him on topic before Jensen comes back, but he goes on.

"It's why Jensen and I are such good friends. Because she wants to be a journalist, so she also needs a good understanding of people. We both really know how to talk to people. Actually—"

"You said your great-grandpa was a tiger hunter," I blurt.

He frowns. "Well, I didn't say that, *exactly*. I'm not supposed to talk about stuff like that. . . ."

"How did he do it?"

Ricky stares at me, silent, for once.

"I mean, hypothetically. Obviously not *actually*. But, like, if someone *were* to catch a tiger."

Ricky nods, trying to make sense of me. "Right. You're really into tigers, aren't you? But tigers are majestic creatures, and they're endangered. They really shouldn't be hunted."

"Oh, I know, yeah, definitely. I'm not going to. But if I *were* going to . . ." I'm talking so quickly that I'm afraid I might scare him, but Ricky doesn't seem too alarmed.

He shrugs. "Well, I don't really know the details. I never knew my great-grandfather, and my family doesn't really talk about that part of his life, so who knows?"

Disappointment slices straight through me. Obviously he doesn't know. This was such a stupid idea. I thought I could be a hero, that I could actually help. But I'm just me.

I try to hold all my emotions inside, so Ricky can't see, but I feel a hot rush of tears building behind my eyes. I squeeze them shut and try to breathe.

"Oh no," Ricky says, shifting in his seat, looking horrified by my reaction. "I can still help, maybe! Do you like hunting or something?"

I shake my head, trying to get myself under control. I need to get out of this situation and go home and think up a plan B. "Not hunting, really. I just wanted to know how to catch a tiger, I guess. But I was just curious. It's not a big deal. I'm gonna go."

"Wait! Don't go. You look so . . ." He pauses, cheeks going pink.

"Never mind," I say, just as he says—

"I know!" He reaches into his backpack and pulls out a thin, colorful magazine. No, not a magazine. A comic book. I lean closer to read the title: *The Adventures of Superman: Doom Trap!*

Ricky grins. "We could make a trap. Like a pit to catch tigers in. It'll be so cool, see?" He opens the comic to a dog-eared page and shows me the drawing of Superman, trapped in a giant metal box and a web of red laser beams.

"I don't think I can do something like that. And also . . ." I stare at the illustration. "Isn't Superman the good guy? Doesn't he break out of that trap?"

Ricky frowns, and now he's the one who looks disappointed. "Oh, yeah. I guess. I just meant . . ." He looks down and stuffs the comic book back into his bag. "Sorry, I know this wasn't what you were looking for. My dad's always telling me I get too excited about things, and my friends don't really get it when I talk about comics and stuff, so yeah, I understand if you think it's weird."

And now I feel guilty for causing this whole situation in the first place. "It's not weird. It's just . . ." I stop myself before I say, *It's just not what I was looking for.*

Because, actually, a tiger trap is exactly what I was looking for. Obviously, I can't build a trap out of metal and lasers. Obviously, it's ridiculous to use a comic book as a how-to guide—but not as ridiculous as trying to *trap a magical talking tiger.*

Ricky is someone who makes things happen. He acts without overthinking. If I want to catch a tiger, I need to be more like him. "Actually, say I don't have steel and lasers. Do you think I could build a trap with normal stuff?"

His eyebrows shoot way up. "Wait, are we actually building a tiger trap?"

I clear my throat. "Well, *me,* not *we,* and I don't know—"

He wiggles with excitement. "If you're making the tiger trap here, I *have* to do it with you."

I shake my head. I don't want to disappoint him again, but . . . "I don't think that's a good idea. . . ."

He leans forward, nearly falling out of his chair. "Lily, I *have* to. That sounds so fun. And besides, I know way more than you do. I read *so many comic books,* and plus, I've probably inherited knowledge from my great-grandpa, like in my blood or something. I will be an excellent resource!"

I bite my lip. It's not that I don't want to be his friend. It's just that most people probably wouldn't understand the whole magical talking tiger part of this. "I don't know, Ricky. . . ."

He droops. "Oh, well, that's okay, then. You don't have to invite me if you don't want to."

Now I'm really hoping for Jensen to come back, but

she's still in the staff room, and I have to stand here, feeling way guilty.

Maybe inviting him wouldn't be so bad. I don't have to tell him what the trap is *actually* for. And maybe it would be nice to have some help—from someone who isn't all that bothered by the *why* of things.

"Fine," I say, and his whole body goes electric, sitting straight up.

"*Really?* I'm so excited. This is gonna be EPIC." He makes an explosion gesture to show *epic.* "I'm so glad you said yes. Because now making a tiger trap is in my head and it *will not leave.*"

"Right," I say.

"I have to stop by home to get supplies after tutoring, but I'll be at your house as soon as possible. Jensen said you live across the street, right?"

"You mean . . . today?" I ask. "Don't you have to ask your dad?"

"Oh, he won't notice I'm gone." He tears a piece of paper out of his notebook and scribbles his phone number, but before he can hand it to me, Jensen comes back with the pudding.

Ricky hides the scrap of paper in his fist, and I shoot him a *Be quiet!* look. He nods and mimes zipping his lips shut. He tries to look serious, but his big grin busts out, and he practically radiates excitement.

Jensen frowns. "What's going on here?"

"Nothing," Ricky and I say at once, which is probably a little suspicious.

Jensen's about to grill us more, but something stops her. She looks over my shoulder and her eyebrows rise. I turn to follow her gaze.

Sam's standing behind me, arms folded across her chest, glaring at me with her black-rimmed eyes. She's angry.

17

Jensen speaks first. Her eyes flicker from surprise to confusion to curiosity. "Hi," she says. "I'm Jensen." She gives Sam the same warm, inviting smile she gave me—only with something extra, something curious and almost hopeful—maybe because Sam is her age. Jensen tucks a dark curl behind her ear, and her lucky freckles glow.

I can't help but feel jealous, because it feels like without even trying, Sam stole my friend. That's the problem with sticky people.

"H-hey," Sam says to Jensen, stammering a little bit. "I'm, uh, Sam." She's caught off guard by Jensen's niceness or something. But then she turns back to me, eyes narrowing. She stands a little taller. Sam's most comfortable in her anger. "Why did you run out in the middle of our conversation? You can't just *do* that."

I swallow, feeling Jensen's and Ricky's eyes on us. I want to disappear, but my invisibility switch isn't working. It's been malfunctioning lately.

"Why didn't you just *tell* me where you were going?" Sam asks.

"I . . ." I'm not sure what to say. *Because I couldn't tell you about my secret tiger plan?* "I had to come here." The words kerplunk at my feet, falling flat.

An awkward silence echoes, until Jensen exclaims, "Oh, I know you!"

Sam's eyes widen, and Jensen grins. "Not to be creepy or anything. You just looked familiar to me. You went to Sun Elementary, right? Like, ages ago?"

Sam pauses. Her cheeks go pink. "Um, yeah, for a few years. We lived here—yeah, a while ago. Ages ago."

I stare at my sister. I've never seen her stumble over her words like that. She's normally so sure of herself. And so . . . mean. Now all her edges go soft.

Jensen toys with her curls. "You know, we're doing a bake sale to raise money for the library. It was Lily's idea, actually. And you're welcome to help, if you're interested. I can give you my number and we can coordinate."

"Yeah, I . . . okay. I've—yeah." Sam readjusts her shirt, even though it looked fine.

I glance at Ricky, but he's just eating his second pudding, completely oblivious to any strangeness.

Pass me your number while they're distracted, I say with my eyes.

In response, he points to his cup and gives me a thumbs-up, as if I was wondering how his pudding was.

I take a very deep breath and exhale slowly, like Mom does when she's dealing with Halmoni.

Jensen grins. "That would be *awesome*!" she says as she takes Sam's phone and types her number in. I feel a pang of jealousy because *Sam* just got someone's phone number, no problem, like everything is easy for her.

Jensen and Sam stare at each other for a few seconds, and it's like Sam has forgotten about me completely.

I start to feel antsy. "Anyway," I mumble. I stare at Ricky. Silently I tell him, *Give me your number now, super subtle.*

"Oh, yeah!" Ricky says. He holds out the scrap of paper and drops it into my palm. He lowers his voice to a loud whisper. "For later. You know. For the *secret plan.*"

Jensen looks surprised. Sam looks suspicious.

I take another deep breath and force a very normal smile. "Okay, well, we should go," I say.

"Right!" Jensen says. "I'm sorry, I didn't mean to hold you up. Anyway, Ricky and I really need to get back to tutoring."

Ricky shakes his head. "It's okay, Jensen. I can see you're making a friend. And I want to be *respectful* of that."

Jensen laughs, and Sam gives an awkward goodbye shrug before dragging me away from the table.

Ricky calls after us, mouth full of pudding. "See you later!"

I wave goodbye as Sam pulls me out of the library, and when we're out, I turn to her. "You didn't have to embarrass me like that."

She stares at me. "Seriously? That's what you're upset about? You ran out in the middle of a conversation and left me with Mom, who's already super stressed."

"Sorry," I murmur, and I mean it. I'm still annoyed with Sam, but about this, she's kind of right.

"I don't know. I get it. I'm mad, too. I'm mad that it's happening, and I'm even madder that Mom didn't tell us sooner." Sam runs a hand over her face. "Being in that house, it's like a prison. Sometimes I want to run away."

I wish I could explain that I wasn't running away. That I have a plan, that it's all going to be okay. But she's made it very clear that she doesn't believe in the magic.

As we hike back up the stairs, I squint at the house, trying to see what Sam sees. To me, the house has always been a safe place. It protects us.

But I guess I can almost see it, in the way the nearly-black vines strangle the house, the way the door shuts and locks. The way the house hides, tucked away in the trees. I can see it—almost—this house as a prison.

Or even as a trap.

18

Ricky arrives on his bike a few hours later, after Mom takes Halmoni to a follow-up doctor's appointment. Sam's upstairs, so it's just me in the living room, which is probably good, because he's got about a thousand yards of rope wrapped around his waist and is wearing head-to-toe camouflage—including a camo-patterned top hat.

"Whoa," I say as he steps through the front door.

He lifts his top hat in greeting. "Tiger Trapmaster, at your service."

I blink. "What?"

"Yeah, you're right. The name needs some work." He walks past me, unties the rope, and dumps it onto my living room floor. When he sees my confusion, he clarifies: "My superhero name, obviously."

"Right." I feel bad, because I know he's having fun, and I don't want him to think I'm mocking him, but also—this isn't a *game.* This matters. A lot. "I don't think the camo is necessary?"

He grins. "It's not. But it's *cool.* What's your superhero name?"

"I'm not a superhero." I pick up the rope, trying to change the subject. "What do we do with this?"

He squints at me. "Well, fine, but at least wear this." He lifts the top hat from his head and places it on mine. Then he nods, satisfied. "That's better."

The brim of the hat is a little sweaty, and a little big. "Why do you have a camo top hat?"

He tilts his head. "What do you mean?"

I blink. After knowing him for a couple of days, it's obvious that he has a lot of strange hats. But maybe he doesn't think they're strange at all. To him, a camo top hat is perfectly normal.

"The hat is just . . ." I'm about to say *kind of weird,* but I remember his face at the grocery store, and I stop myself. I don't want to make him feel bad like that. "It's unique," I finish, and then, before we can dive deeper into this hat conversation, I try to refocus. "I was thinking we should set the trap over here. Follow me."

I lead him to the basement door.

"This place is so intense," he says, taking in the herbs, the charms, the little statues—and of course, the boxes and chests, still stacked by the basement door.

"It's not *intense,*" I tell him, bristling a little. Maybe I shouldn't have been so nice about the hat. "It's my home."

He turns pink. "Sorry. I like it, though. It's like being in a thrift store, or a not-scary haunted house."

Before I can respond, Sam's footsteps creak down the stairs, and she stops in front of us. "Excuse me," she says, folding her arms over her chest and raising an eyebrow at me. "Why is he here and what's on your head?"

"Oh," I say. "This is a top hat." Honestly, there's not much more to say about it. "And Ricky's just here to . . . read."

Sam frowns, glancing at the rope, at Ricky's camo, and then back at me. "Does Mom know you invited someone over?"

Ricky looks back and forth between us, then clears his throat and smiles at Sam. "Hi, I'm Ricky. I'm Lily's friend from the library."

Sam rolls her eyes, "Yes, I know. I literally just saw you this morning."

Then she pulls me into Halmoni's empty bedroom, where we can talk privately. "You didn't even ask me if you could have a friend over," she says, her voice bordering on exasperation.

I shrug. "Mom won't care. She wants me to make friends."

"Yeah, but you can't just do whatever you want. You have to *ask*. Remember the conversation we *just* had?"

"I'm sorry. He just kind of showed up. He invited himself." It's technically true.

"Don't be so sketchy! I'm not stupid. I know you have some secret plan. Why are you wearing that hat and why are you holding a pile of rope?" Her eyes narrow. "This is about your weird tiger theory, isn't it?"

"No," I lie, unconvincingly.

Sam frowns. "I think I have to tell Mom."

She reaches for her phone, but I grab her wrist to stop her. "Don't, please. Sisters . . . keep each other's secrets."

We stare each other down, until finally, she shakes her head. "Fine. Do whatever. Just leave me out of it."

"Oh." It's what I wanted, I guess. But it still stings because while I don't want her to *stop* me from doing this, I also don't want her to ignore me. I want her to care.

There's an ache in my chest because it should be Sam and me, together, building a tiger trap. This story belongs to sisters. It should be *us*.

But Sam twists her wrist out of my hand before walking out of the bedroom and back up the stairs.

"Your sister seems . . ." Ricky swallows. "Nice?"

I ignore him. "We need to build the trap downstairs."

He frowns. "Well, I've done a lot of Googling, and normally tiger pits are outside. So they can be, you know, a pit."

I push the basement door open and switch on the light, which, thankfully, decides to work today. It flickers once, twice, then stays on, buzzing faintly. "Yeah, but a basement is already kind of like a pit."

Ricky squirms. "But . . . it's not, though."

"I don't want it to get rained on," I say. I can't tell him the real reason—the tiger appeared in the house. She thinks the stolen star stories are somewhere in here. And the basement is the only place where my family won't notice a giant trap.

The excuse is good enough for Ricky, and we head down the stairs to examine our work space.

"You do realize," Ricky says, "that, in theory, you'd be luring a tiger *into your house* and then *into your basement.* Which seems like not the best idea."

"It's hypothetical," I remind him. I try very hard not to think, *Maybe he's right.*

"Right." He nods. He surveys the room and cracks his knuckles. "We need to make a pit, somehow."

"Well . . . ," I say, thinking. "I guess we could maybe use some of those boxes upstairs? And stack them? And then we can use the rope to secure the boxes, so the tiger can't just knock everything over. The *hypothetical* tiger, I mean."

Halmoni said moving the boxes on an unlucky day could be dangerous. But how do I know if today is unlucky?

"Box tower. Yes. Great idea," Ricky says.

I weigh my options. I can't really think of another way to make a trap, so either I move the boxes and hope it's a lucky day, or I don't and I give up on trapping the tiger.

"Just be careful not to break anything," I add. Halmoni said breaking something was the worst thing, so at least I can avoid that.

We get to work. We shove the Korean chests aside, scraping them across the wood floor and clearing a path for the lighter boxes.

Then we carry Halmoni's cardboard boxes down from the top of the stairs and pile them in the basement. Some are light enough that we can carry them individually, but the bigger ones we take together. We walk slowly down the stairs, him holding the front, me carrying the back.

When we're about halfway through the boxes, and maneuvering a particularly heavy one down the stairs, Ricky says, "My mom likes hats, too."

I stop, peering over the big box to look at him. "What?"

He shrugs, shifting the weight between us. "I don't know—you asked about my hat."

"Yeah, like half an hour ago."

"Sorry, I don't like awkward silences."

"Oh," I say. He stares at me like he's waiting for more. "I don't think it was an awkward silence. It was more of a busy silence."

He laughs. "*Busy silence.* I never thought of that before."

We take a few more steps, and he keeps talking. "My mom and I used to buy hats together. That was kind of our thing. You need a good hat for every occasion, because a special hat can make you feel special. It's the same reason superheroes wear capes."

I nod along, but my mind snags on the *used to.* It's like what he said at the grocery store: she *used to* make sticky buns. She *likes* hats, in the present tense, but they *used to* buy hats.

There's a catch in his voice, too, when he mentions his mom. I wonder what that means, if maybe his parents are divorced and he doesn't see her that often.

But I don't ask about it. I don't like when random people ask me about Dad, and I don't want to make Ricky uncomfortable.

"That's a good point," I say instead.

We reach the bottom of the steps and start waddling the heavy box over to the rest of them.

"I have a newsboy cap like from the old days, and a lime-green fedora, and—"

He cuts off abruptly as the cardboard slips from his grasp. I stumble forward, trying to catch it, but it's too heavy, and for the second time, I fall in front of Ricky.

The camo top hat flies off my head, and a horrible clatter rings through the basement as the box hits the ground, followed by a loud *pop* when I land on top of it, crumpling the cardboard and smashing the contents inside.

It's the sound of something breaking.

It's the sound of bad luck.

I freeze, as if by refusing to move I can undo what just happened. I wait for Sam to come running down the stairs, but she doesn't, and it's just me and Ricky and whatever we broke.

Ricky's eyes are wide. "Are you okay? I'm so sorry! I thought I had it, but—"

"I'm fine," I say, scrambling to stand. "I just need to see if we broke something." I turn the box right side up and try to peel off the tape to check inside, but my fingers keep shaking, so it's hard to get a grip. Ricky probably thinks I'm being way overdramatic. He probably thinks I'm the weirdest of weird.

He pushes the hair out of his eyes. "Would you get in trouble for breaking something?"

"Oh, no," I say quickly. But *would* Halmoni be mad? She seemed really upset when Mom tried to move things.

"Here, let me help." Ricky leans over to open the box, and I check inside.

Beneath a layer of Bubble Wrap is a pile of pots and pans.

Everything looks intact.

The clatter must have been the pans banging against each other. And the pop was me crushing the layer of Bubble Wrap.

I let out a hot breath. "Everything's fine," I say, more to myself than to Ricky.

I rearrange the cookware inside the box—but inside the biggest pot, something catches my eye.

I reach in and pull out three wads of Bubble Wrap. The objects inside glint beneath the plastic, flashing in the light.

"Whoa." Ricky sucks in a breath as he leans over my shoulder. "We. Found. *Treasure.*"

Only it isn't treasure. It's . . . jars.

19

"Star jars," I breathe.

I peel the Bubble Wrap off one of them, and the jar inside is small and round, made of dark blue glass, with a silver cork stuffed in its mouth.

Quickly I unwrap the others, checking for cracks, but they're okay, too. One of them is tall and thin, made of clear glass with a black cork. The other is dark green and square shaped.

Ricky takes a step closer. "What's a star jar?"

"Um, nothing." Except they aren't nothing. In fact, these might be *everything*.

Halmoni said she took the star stories and stuffed them into jars. The tiger thought those jars were hidden somewhere in the house. And Halmoni was *super intense* about being careful with the boxes.

This is it. These are the precious jars. The dangerous stories. They have to be.

This is what the tiger wants.

I squint at them, and it might be a trick of the light, but I can almost see something moving inside them—something like smoke, or like magic.

For one overwhelming moment, I want to uncork the jars and hold them to my ear like seashells, so I can hear magic inside, roaring like the ocean.

I want so badly to hear these stories.

"These are my halmoni's." I try to keep my voice steady. "We can just put these on the side, and I'll give them to her later."

Ricky shrugs like it's not a big deal, which I guess, to him, it *isn't*. They're just jars. Regular, normal jars. Totally. I chew my thumbnail and stare at them.

Ricky breaks the silence. "So, what would you do after you trapped the tiger?" And then, like he's afraid I won't answer, he adds, "In *Superman: Doom Trap!*, Lex Luthor wants to torture him to reveal the secrets of Krypton and also the universe—"

"It's not like that," I interrupt, because that kind of makes me sound like the bad guy. "This is real life. This isn't like your comic books, okay?"

Instantly, I feel guilty for snapping. Ricky has been

nice enough to help. It's not his fault he doesn't know the bigger picture, and if he wants to talk about comics or hats or anything, I should just let him. Quieter, I say, "This is just different."

He pauses and gets really focused on readjusting his camo pants. "I'm not getting tutored because I'm stupid. I mean, I'm not stupid."

I fiddle with my braids. "Yeah, I know. You already said that, in the library, and I don't think you are. Lots of people get tutored."

"I'm just saying, in case you think stuff. Or hear stuff about me." He lifts a shoulder like he doesn't care, even though he clearly does.

I sit on one of the boxes. "Hear stuff from *who*?" I don't think I need to point out the obvious: I don't have any friends.

"Yeah, that's true," he says, sitting on the box next to me. "I failed language arts last year."

"Oh," I say.

At my school in California, it was superhard to fail a class. Even if you did badly on all the assignments, as long as you put in the bare minimum effort, the teacher would take pity on you and at least let you pass.

Maybe the school here is way harder, because Ricky doesn't seem like someone who wouldn't try. He's the type of kid who wears head-to-toe camo for a hypothetical tiger hunt. That type of kid tries.

Drumming his fingers against the cardboard, he says, "It's not my fault, though. The teacher was against me. She hated me."

"Okay," I say. "I guess that makes sense."

He looks up at me, surprised. "Really? You believe me?"

I nod. He looks so hopeful, but it's not like I have any reason *not* to believe him. And to be totally honest, I don't really care if he's good at language arts. Grades don't really translate to friendship.

He sighs in relief. "That's good. I didn't want you to think badly of me. Because it's really not my fault. But anyway, that's why I'm getting tutored this summer. If I don't pass a test in a couple of weeks, I'll have to repeat sixth grade."

I try to hide my surprise. Because that's a pretty big deal. And here's what I don't say: From what I've seen, he slacks off a lot during his tutoring sessions. It almost seems like he's trying *not* to learn anything.

It's really none of my business. For some reason, though, he cares about my approval. "I'm sure you'll pass," I say.

He nods. "Yeah. Me too. It'll be fine."

There's an awkward silence, and then he says, "Why

are you really doing this? I mean, I'm as excited as the next kid to build a fake tiger trap, but there must be a reason."

I shrug, avoiding his eyes. "We should get back to work."

"Seriously, though?"

I hesitate, trying to think of a decent lie. I've been keeping so many secrets. And secrets are exhausting.

The truth is, I want to tell the truth. "My halmoni is sick," I tell him. When he looks confused, I clarify: "My grandma."

He blows air from his lips. "I'm sorry. That's awful."

"She's afraid of tigers, so I wanted to make her feel better." It's not quite the truth—but it's close enough. My shoulders loosen, and my lungs fill with relief.

It's nice to talk to somebody.

"That must be scary," he says. "Even if it is just in her head."

I swallow up the words *You have no idea.* And I nod. "It is."

"That's really cool of you to do," he says. "You're the coolest girl I've ever been friends with."

"Oh." I didn't know he considered us friends, but it's kind of nice to hear.

It feels like, maybe, he could be a real friend—one who sticks.

"So." He stands, brushing off his pants. "Do you have any raw meat?"

"Wait, what?"

"According to the internet, the most important part of the tiger trap is the bait. Most tiger hunters used raw meat, like beef or—"

"Well, it's hypothetical, so . . . we won't do that," I say.

He nods. "Right, yeah. That makes sense."

"Let's just finish the trap."

He leans over, picks up the top hat, and hands it back to me. "Let's do this."

I smile as we get back to work. We pay more attention now—taking each box step by step, careful and slow—leaving only the heaviest ones and the big Korean chests upstairs. Once we've got enough boxes downstairs, we start arranging them in a ring, stacking the lighter boxes on the heavier ones.

It's like a giant puzzle, and even though it's important, even though this really, really matters . . . it's also *fun*.

Once we're done, we wrap the rope around the boxes, though we're not really sure quite what to do. I tie five knots, just to be safe.

Finally, we step back to admire our handiwork.

"Nicely done, Tiger Trapmaster," I say.

Ricky's smile fills his whole face. "Likewise, Super Tiger Girl."

"I'm not a superhero," I say automatically. Except Super Tiger Girl does sound cooler than Invisible Girl, and it feels kind of nice to be *super.*

Before he leaves, I lift his top hat off my head and hand it to him. I'm pretty sure I have hat hair, with some strands sweat-stuck to my forehead and others standing straight up. "Don't forget this," I say.

He shrugs. "Keep it for now. Just in case you find a *hypothetical* tiger. I'll get it back when we hang out again."

"Hang out? To do what?" I'm not sure what he thinks comes next, but this is pretty much it. The trap is finished.

He stares at me like it's obvious. "We're friends now. Friends hang out."

I blink. "Oh, okay. Yeah."

And then I start to smile. Because I really would like to hang out again. Somehow, he made trapping a tiger fun.

I say goodbye to Ricky, and as soon as he's gone, I take the star jars up to the attic room and hide them under my bed. Sam's in the shower, thankfully, so she doesn't bother me, and I lie on my stomach, on the floor, staring at the jars.

They seem like regular jars, almost. But even under the bed, they seem to glow.

Raw meat won't work, because magical tigers play by different rules. But looking at these jars, I realize: I've found my bait.

20

"What are you doing?" The floorboards creak behind me, and I turn to see Sam in her pajamas.

"Nothing," I say, jumping to my feet.

I'm full of jittery energy. Beneath the bed, the star jars wait.

But I glance at the clock. It's only evening. I still have hours before everyone's asleep—before I can sneak a jar downstairs and bait the tiger.

Sam narrows her eyes. She takes a breath, like there's something she wants to ask, but then shakes her head.

It's not like Sam to hold her questions in, and I don't know if I'm grateful, or sad.

When she opens her mouth again, she seems to change her mind, asking a different question instead. "What's the deal with that boy?"

"He's helping me . . . do something." I can't help but smile a little when I add, "He's my friend."

She raises an eyebrow, and her lips lift into that *I know something you don't* smirk. "Your friend?"

My cheeks get hot when I realize what she means. "It's not like that."

Her voice is teasing. "Not like what?"

"Not like how you're acting."

Sam laughs. Apparently my embarrassment puts her in a good mood.

Then her eyes soften a little, and she points to the floor in front of the mirror. "Sit down. If you have a crush, you should learn how to do your hair."

"I'm fine the way I am," I say. "And it's not a crush." I don't know how to deal with Sam. One minute she hates me, the next she wants to have a Sister Moment.

More importantly, I don't have time for hair. I have an actual lifesaving mission to go on.

But she keeps pointing, refusing to take no for an answer. And I guess I have to wait a few hours anyway.

When I give up and sit in front of the mirror, Sam kneels behind me. She unravels my braids, twisting the strands, weaving them together in a new way.

As she works, my jitteriness fades, replaced by this quieter, deeper wanting. I want to tell her about the tiger and the star jars and the trap.

But I'm afraid her teeth will go sharp and she'll call me crazy, so I hold my breath until the wanting goes away.

After a few minutes, Sam asks, "When did you meet Jensen?"

It's a random question, and not really what I want to talk about, but it's way better than talking about Ricky.

"At the library, when we first got here," I tell her. "She's really nice. She gave me a cupcake. And the library doesn't look like a haunted gingerbread house anymore." I clamp my lips shut. Too much—the gingerbread thing was a weird comment. I change the subject. "Do you remember her from elementary school?"

Sam shrugs, tugging on my hair just a little. "I mean, yeah, the school was pretty small. But she was a year older, so I didn't think she noticed me at all." She pauses, then adds, "Not that I'm saying she *noticed* me. Just, yeah."

"Yeah," I say, feeling awkward without really knowing why. I feel like she wants me to say something, but I have no idea what.

Sam finishes my braids, pulling bobby pins from her own hair and sticking them against my skull, until she leans back, looking at me in the mirror.

Instead of two braids framing my face, my hair is twisted into a braided crown, with wispy strands hanging around my ears.

With my new hair and Halmoni's pendant around my neck, I look like a princess. Or more—a warrior-princess.

I'm not used to seeing myself like this. "I don't look like the girl in the tiger story anymore," I whisper, more to myself than to Sam.

Sam hasn't looked like the girl in that story for years, ever since she cut her hair to her shoulders and got that white streak. But I've always worn my braids. I've always been Little Eggi.

Sam groans. "Enough with the tiger story, Lily. That story is the worst."

I don't understand what she's saying. We loved the sister story. We ran into Halmoni's room every night. *Tell us the story about the sun and the moon.* "What do you mean?"

"Well, first of all," Sam starts, "the sisters are stupid. A tiger is scratching at their door. It's *clearly* not their halmoni. Why can't they see that?"

"Because he's dressed up in—"

"And also, the older sister goes on and on about protecting the younger sister, and then she goes and opens the window for the tiger."

I lean back. "The older sister doesn't open the window. The *younger* sister opens the door."

Sam shakes her head. "No, that's not right."

"It *is*. That's how the story goes." In the story, the tiger picks the little sister. She's the one it calls to. She's the one who answers. She's the special one.

I'm not sure why Sam is so confused. I tell her, "Eggi opens the door, the tiger chases them, and when they tell a story, the sky god saves them."

"No." Something in Sam's voice scares me. A sharp edge that wasn't there before. "The sisters end up on opposite ends of the sky, and they can't even talk to one another. They see each other every day, but only to wave hello and goodbye. They're alone."

I pull my knees into my chest. "It's not sad. It's happy. The sisters escape the tiger. They're safe forever."

But now I'm not so sure.

"The whole point is that it's a sad story, Lily. All those old fairy tales are meant to scare kids. It's a lesson. You know: don't open the door for strangers. And: run from danger."

Silence swells in the room, filling every crack in the creaky wood. I clear my throat and force words out. "What if the sisters didn't run?"

Sam sighs. "What do you mean?"

"If it were your story, if a tiger was chasing you . . . would you run or would you . . . face it?"

She hesitates. "You're not talking about the stories being real again, are you, because—"

"No, no," I say quickly. "That was a mental stress reaction. I know. I mean it hypothetically."

Silence, until Sam barks a laugh. It's so startling that it frightens a laugh out of me, too. For a second, my anxiety eases, and her laugh is a bright spot in the darkness.

"Lily! Are you kidding me? I would run! Tigers, you know, *eat people.*"

"Yeah," I say. She's right. That's the reality of what I'm facing, and I can't tell her about it.

Sam gets up and flops back onto the bed, and I assume this talk is over. Sam doesn't end conversations anymore. She just escapes them.

But a few minutes later, she says, "If it were me in the story, I don't know. I don't know if I'd run. I'd want to do the brave thing. It's just, in that scenario, I'm not really sure what the brave thing is."

21

Carefully, I pull the square green star jar out from under my bed. Sam is asleep. The whole house is asleep. And I am ready.

As quietly as possible, I slide open the drawer where I've hidden Halmoni's mugwort. I break off a piece and slip it into my pocket. I clasp Halmoni's pendant around my neck. And finally, I lift Ricky's hat from my dresser and place it on my head.

Because you never know. Maybe it will help. Maybe it will make me special. Maybe it will turn me into a hero.

Holding the star jar and wearing my protection, I tiptoe out of the attic room and down the stairs. I call on my invisibility, and the night wraps me in shadows. The sound of rain cloaks my footsteps.

Everybody else sleeps as I creep past Halmoni's room, past Mom on the couch, toward the basement.

"Am I making the right decision?" I whisper to the corked jar.

No response. Even the house is still tonight, like it's waiting for my next move.

I turn the basement door's knob, and the door swings open, inviting me in.

This time, I won't be afraid. Halmoni faced tigers once, and now I will, too.

I am Lily, and I am brave. I am my halmoni's granddaughter.

I am not hunted by tigers.

I am the hunter.

And a tiger is no match for me.

I hold the jar—the bait—in my hands, and I sit on the stairs with my back to the door, looking down at the boxes.

I wait.

* * *

I don't mean to fall asleep, but apparently I do, because I wake up to a rustling.

I spring to my feet, and as soon as I see my trap, I'm filled with a shock of excitement and panic—because I *did* it. But also: *I did it*—and now there's a tiger, in my basement. Trapped.

With one hand, I grab the star jar. With the other, I pinch my leg, just to be sure. But this is not a dream and it's not a hallucination.

Surrounded by my ring of boxes, the tiger sits back on her hind legs, still except for her tail flicking back and forth. The moonlight spills through the window, making her black stripes look almost silver, and she's even bigger than I remembered—almost too big for my trap.

"Amusing," she says flatly. She looks annoyed but unconcerned.

I keep my distance, staying where I am in the middle of the staircase, looking down at her. One of the tiger facts flashes through my brain: *A tiger's tooth can cut through bone!*

But so does another one: *If you look a tiger in the eye, it's less likely to kill you.*

I force myself to stare into those glowing yellow eyes, those pupils like pools of black ink. I stand taller, acting braver than I am. "You found my trap," I say, deepening my voice so I sound older.

The tiger's lips curl into a smile. "I will admit, I was not expecting this."

I clear my throat. "You said you could heal my halmoni. Now that you are trapped, I demand that you help her."

"Interesting. I wouldn't have considered you the type.

Unfortunately for you, I am not trapped. I am merely . . . testing you." She picks a dried herb from her sharp teeth. "Nice mugwort, by the way."

I feel for the mugwort in my pocket, but it's gone—and in a flash of orange and black, the tiger disappears, too. My trap is empty.

"Tigers do not give in to demands. . . ." Her voice comes from behind me, and I spin around to see her standing in the doorway, at the top of the stairs.

She's so much bigger than me, and she steps forward, forcing me down one step. Then another. And another and another until I am in the basement, pressed up against my own wall of boxes. Silly, to think I could trick a tiger. Silly, silly, little girl, and now—

"But we do offer deals." Her voice is more curious than menacing, somewhere between a growl and a whisper. "I told you I would only offer once, but for you, Super Tiger Girl, perhaps I will make an exception. Perhaps I will offer a new deal, one that's a little more fun."

The star jar is slippery in my damp palms, and I squeeze it tighter. "What's your offer?"

"You return the stories, your halmoni feels better. But here's the fun part: in order to return the stories to the sky, I must tell them." She flashes her teeth. "And stories are always better with an audience."

I take a deep breath. Part of me wants to hear the

stories. But Halmoni said they were bad. And they *made* people bad, because everyone who heard them felt pain.

"The stories are dangerous," I say.

"They are powerful."

"You said they have the power to change someone." I shudder, and for some reason I think of Halmoni, throwing up in the bathroom. How, for just a moment, she looked like a monster.

The tiger's eyes glint in the dark. "This is my offer. Take it or leave it."

I've got about twenty layers of fear stacked over my heart right now. Fear of saying the wrong thing. Fear of doing the wrong thing. Fear of hurting Halmoni. Fear of not saving Halmoni. Fear of a magical talking tiger.

But if I peel back all those layers—there's something else, burning deep inside me. There's that tiger-hunting fierceness, and I imagine myself grabbing that feeling, gripping so hard it hurts.

I am small, but I am not easy prey.

I clear the whispers from my throat, and when I speak, my voice is strong. "Will releasing the star stories really make Halmoni feel better?"

"Of course." Her eyes flash in a way that tells me her promises mean nothing. "Open the jars, listen to a story, heal your halmoni. That is painfully reasonable."

The jar feels hot in my hands. Upstairs, it glowed

faintly, but now it's like holding a lantern. Maybe the light from the small basement window catches the jar just right, or maybe my eyes play tricks. Or maybe it's magic inside the jar, waking up after sleeping for so long. What I thought were dust motes in the jar look like stars now—an entire miniature galaxy, captured in glass.

"I don't trust you." I have to say that, just for the record. I have to say it because I know: I'm going to do it anyway.

I'm sick of being a QAG, too afraid to do anything. For once I want to be the hero.

"Come on," she purrs. "What do you say? Do you accept?"

I grip the jar tighter as I brace myself. "Yes."

Her sharp teeth glow.

And I open the jar.

22

The cork slips from the jar with a loud pop. Then, softer, a hissing sound.

The starlight in the jar seems to spill out, a whole Milky Way tipping over the edge, and the tiger moves closer. She closes her eyes, presses her whiskers against the rim—and drinks the stars.

The basement dances with color, deep blue and orange and purple, and for a second, I can almost hear the roar of an ocean. I can almost taste the scent of the sea.

As the tiger drinks, the glass in my hand gets lighter and lighter until it feels like air. And when she finishes, she steps back, smacking her lips.

"Ah," she says, "I have missed that one."

Then she begins.

* * *

Long, long ago, when man walked like tiger, when nights were dark as ink, long before the sun and the moon and even the stars—there was a girl born of two worlds. She had two sets of skin and she could shift as she pleased: tiger to human, human to tiger.

She loved her magic, and she loved both worlds equally. The problem was, she had to keep it secret. The world around her was divided in two—humans didn't trust tigers, and tigers didn't trust humans, and neither wanted a traitor sleeping in their caves.

So the girl of two worlds lived two lives. By day, she was human. By night, she was tiger. But this, I'm afraid, is an exhausting way to live.

Tigers are wild, out of control. They speak the truth and swallow the world. They are always wanting more. But human girls, she was told, are not meant for wanting. They are meant for helping. They are meant for quiet.

And sometimes, the tiger-girl would mix up her lives. She would feel the wrong things at the wrong time. Too much feeling as a human, too much fear as a tiger. It would be much easier to be only one thing.

Even worse, her secret made her lonely. She had friends and family in both forms, but nobody knew her true heart.

What a terrible way to live, *she thought. But she lived that way anyway. She carried her secret, locked away inside her, until one day, her body shifted and changed in a new way: she was going to have a baby.*

A baby born of two worlds. Born with the same magic—the same curse.

But the tiger-girl, now a tiger-mother, knew what she had to do. She wouldn't let her child live a life split in two. So the tiger-girl asked her human mother to protect the baby, and left to climb the tallest mountain, up and up, until she reached the sky god.

I have never once complained, *she told him,* but I am doing this for my daughter. I am asking you to spare her. Take away her magic. Turn us both human and lock our tiger side away.

The sky god was not pleased. He does not typically grant favors. But she begged and begged. So the sky god said, Yes, fine. I will grant your wish. I can take away your magic, and your baby's, but first . . . hmm . . . your baby must live alone in a cave for one hundred days, without the sun. Oh, and she can only eat mugwort.

The tiger-girl was horrified. She wouldn't trap her baby in a cave! Was there another way? Please, please, please. *She begged and begged some more.*

The sky god was annoyed. What a difficult woman. But

he figured this whole situation was kind of his fault. He'd accidentally given her a second skin. So he said, Yes, fine. There is another way. I will lock away your daughter's magic in exchange for your help.

If you must know, I am getting old. (I mean, of course, I am still smart and strong and handsome, et cetera.) But one day, I will need someone to replace me.

Come live as a sky princess, in my sky castle, and learn my magic. In return, I will grant your wish.

So the tiger-girl agreed, and the sky god, oh so generous, gave her one last day with her daughter.

The tiger-girl was sad to leave her baby, but she knew her child would be safe. Her daughter would never be lost and lonely in her secrets.

Before she left, the tiger-girl hugged her baby goodbye and cried and cried, and when the last tear fell from her eye, it turned into a pearl—a final goodbye, a pendant for her daughter to wear, right above her heartbone.

Goodbye, *she whispered,* and be safe.

Then she had to go. The sky god sent down a rope (or a staircase—it depends who you ask), and she climbed up and up, into her castle.

Living in the sky kingdom is expensive, so the tiger-girl found a job: the night was very dark, and somebody needed to light it.

* * *

When the tiger is done, the night seems a notch brighter, as if there's one more star in the sky. But I could be imagining it.

The tiger licks her lips, slurping up bits of stardust. Her eyes close, as if she's savoring it.

I can't quite explain the way the story settled in my chest. I know what it's like to carry a tiger secret, unable to tell my family because it would scare them. And I feel like the story lit up a piece of me, a piece I thought was hidden.

I don't know how I feel about that, but I know how I feel about something else: I hate that the tiger-girl left her baby. "What if the baby needed her? She could have figured out another way. She didn't *have* to go."

"You're angry," the big cat says softly.

"I'm not . . . I don't . . ." I feel silly, because it's just a story. I know it shouldn't affect me so much, and I don't know why it did. Maybe this is what Halmoni meant by a bad story.

"It's okay," she says, "to feel out of control."

"Why did Halmoni want to hide this story?" My fingers find the pendant around my neck, and I pinch it tight. "Is this pearl . . . was that about her? Was that *her* story?"

"Little one, this is an ancient story. Do not worry about who it once belonged to. It belongs to the sky now—for

all of us to see." There's something sad and lost in her voice. Something that says there's more to the story. I try to read her, but when she tilts her head, her eyes fall into shadow. In the dark, they are unknowable, like a night without stars.

I spin the necklace between the pads of my fingers, feeling like there's something I'm missing. "So, what now? Will Halmoni feel better?"

"Eventually," she says, "but not yet. We've only just begun, and there are consequences to telling the truth."

I pause. "I thought you said this would help her."

"The truth is always painful, especially when it's been hidden so long. There are bound to be unexpected complications." She shrugs, trying to look casual, but her muscles are tense as they ripple beneath her fur. "Anyway, bring me the next star jar tomorrow, at two a.m., and I will tell you another story. Oh, and bring some rice cakes, too. It's the least you can do, if we must meet in this stuffy basement."

"Wait," I say, "what consequences? What if I don't like them? What if I change my mind?" I realize, now, that I've agreed to something I don't understand.

She licks her lips again. "I'm afraid you don't have a choice. You've already released the story. You've heard the beginning, but your halmoni can't heal until we reach the end."

She turns away from me and walks back up the stairs. The steps don't creak beneath her—it's like she's made of air. "It will get worse before it gets better, Little Egg," she says without looking back. "But if you do what I say, it *will* get better. Trust me."

23

The next afternoon, I announce, "I need to make rice cakes."

When I walk downstairs, Mom and Halmoni are sitting together at the dining table, and I join them, plopping myself into a chair. I try to smile like, *Ha ha. Normal. No tigers here.*

"Oh, yes," Halmoni says. "That sound good, little one. We make that later."

"Or, um, now? What about now?"

Sam's sprawled out on the couch, cell phone hovering in front of her face, but she glances over at me with a raised eyebrow. I ignore her.

Mom takes a breath and plasters a grin on her face. "Actually, I was thinking we should all go out today. It would be nice to get out of the house and do something. As a family."

"We could make rice cakes as a family," I say. "Halmoni can teach us how."

Mom's fake smile gets even faker. "Lily. That sounds so fun. Maybe *after* we go out."

Sam lowers her phone. "Mom's obsessed with going out because Halmoni keeps bugging her about the boxes."

Mom clears her throat. "That's not—"

But Halmoni says to me, "You mother move boxes yesterday. I tell her no good. I tell her spirits no like. But of course, she don't listen."

I dig my nails into my palms and nod, even though I feel like there's a giant sign above my head that says, IT WAS ME.

"Anyway," Mom says through a gritted smile, "that's not why. I just thought it would be nice because Halmoni was saying how *good* she felt today."

Now that Mom mentions it, Halmoni does look good. She's curled her hair, and she's even wearing a pop of pink lipstick, which she hasn't done in a while.

But that only makes me want to bake *now,* before she needs to rest again.

Sam shrugs. "Can we go to lunch at that Asian restaurant, on the corner of Willow and Vine?"

I turn to give Sam the stink-eye. Somehow, she's only interested in doing stuff as a family when it conflicts with *my* plans.

Mom frowns. "Uh, really? Why?"

"I'm in the mood," Sam says.

"That place is just a little . . ." Mom makes a face like she's smelling rotten garlic but trying to be polite about it. "Well, it's not authentic."

"Yeah," I chime in. "So we should stay—"

Sam interrupts, "Mom, I'm just saying. I'm just suggesting. I'm just *trying* to spend time with my family."

Mom sighs. "Okay, fine. As long as Halmoni's okay with it."

I get this sudden balloon-pop urge to cry, but Halmoni claps her hands and smiles. "Yes, good! They have the best sweet-sour. My favorite."

So I'm outnumbered, and we all get ready to go.

But as we pile into the car, Halmoni turns to me. "Later I teach you rice cakes," she whispers. "I promise."

The restaurant sign says DRAGON THYME! in red curlicue letters, and two stone lions sit by the doors, guarding the entrance.

"I haven't been here in ages," Mom says as she ushers us inside.

"They have good sweet-sour," Halmoni reminds us, and Mom sighs.

Inside, the walls are lined with shoji screens painted with pink cherry blossoms. Red paper lanterns hang from the ceiling, and a gold cat statue sits in the corner, waving *Hello! Hello!*

But I'm fixated on the painting right above the hostess stand. It's a classic Korean painting of a tiger, with eyes as big and round as rice cakes. It looks like it's laughing.

Suddenly I feel sweaty. It's too hot in here.

"Sam," Mom hisses, "what are you doing?"

I glance over at my sister, who's nervously scanning the entire restaurant, all jittery in her skin, like she's looking for something—only I can't tell if she wants to find it or she's afraid to.

"Nothing," Sam snaps, turning as red as the lanterns.

For a second I wonder if she's looking for the tiger, but no. I don't let myself hope.

A girl, probably around Sam's age, walks over to us. She's got chopsticks stuck in her blond hair and big, round, chocolate-chip-cookie eyes. "Hi! I'm Olivia and I'll be taking care of you today! This way to your table!"

When she leads us through the restaurant, I catch disappointment on Sam's face, but it flits away fast.

Olivia sits us down and hands out menus, and Halmoni orders sweet-and-sour pork, sweet-and-sour shrimp, and sweet-and-sour beef. Just to start.

As soon as Olivia's out of earshot, Sam says, "It's like an Asian stereotype vomited all over this place."

Then she looks at Halmoni. And swallows. And studies her menu very hard.

I think of Halmoni throwing up on the road and study my own menu, even though I'm not reading any of the sashimi options.

"I haven't been here since the nineties, and it hasn't gotten much better," Mom says. "But, man, this brings back memories."

I ask, *Are you happy that you left? Do you regret leaving? Do you regret coming back?*

But only silently, in my head.

Halmoni laughs and wags her finger. "Oh, you mother in the nineties."

Mom raises her eyebrows at Halmoni. "Excuse me?"

Halmoni giggles. "*So* troublemaker."

Mom tries to look annoyed but ends up smiling. "Okay, whatever you say."

I look back and forth between them. Halmoni said that before, but I still can't picture it. Mom loves rules. "What did she do?" I ask. "How did she get into trouble?"

Mom laughs. "Halmoni is being overdramatic, as usual."

I sneak a look at my sister, and it's a coin-flip moment: Are we on the same side or different?

Sam leans forward. "Come on, Halmoni, tell us Mom Stories." Then she flashes a small smile at me, and my heart fills up.

I think the tiger was wrong about *consequences,* because this is the happiest my family has been since we moved here.

Halmoni whispers to Sam and me, "So many boyfriends."

"Mom had a lot of boyfriends?" I ask.

Mom *pffts*. "No, I did not."

Halmoni *tsks*. "So many. Always sneaking out to see them."

Sam makes a choking noise, and for the first time, I wonder about Sam dating. I've never thought of her having boyfriends.

Mom clears her throat. "First of all, that's not true. And *Halmoni* was the troublemaker. You know, she made your poor father eat mud."

"What?" Sam asks. Normally, when someone mentions Dad, Sam turns shadowy, but right now she just looks surprised. Interested. Like telling stories about Dad is something fun, instead of something terrible.

"Mud good for him," Halmoni says. Her eyes are happy and sad at the same time, in the missing-him way. "He always talking story—so much talking, but no thinking, aii-yah. Mud help to keep him grounded, think before he speak."

Mom snorts. "It was horrible."

"I make a milkshake for him," Halmoni says. "A milkshake with *little bit* mud mixed in. But he take you mom away. That is bad. Little bit mud? Not that bad."

Sam raises an eyebrow at me like, *Can you believe?* And I furrow mine back like, *Halmoni is wild.*

"What happened?" I ask. "Could he taste it? Did he know?"

Ignoring my question, Mom turns to Halmoni. "He didn't take me away. I went to college."

Halmoni leans forward and whispers loudly, laying on the guilt. "She suppose to come back after, but he take her. She leave poor little Halmoni for a white man. But you mother too little to know better."

Mom's jaw ripples. "Nobody took me away," she repeats. "I left on my own. I wanted to leave." As soon as she says it, she swallows, like she wants to rewind her words. But she can't. No take-backs.

The happy family moment evaporates. I look at Sam, but she's busy rubbing her chopsticks together like she's going to start a fire and burn everything down.

Olivia arrives with our sweet-and-sour dishes. "Here's your starters!" she chirps. "Are you ready to order entrees?"

"We'll need another minute," Mom says with her classic fake smile.

Olivia bobble-head-nods and leaves.

We stare at the food for a few long seconds, until Mom says, "Might as well eat," and leans forward, scooping some shrimp to serve us.

"No, no!" Halmoni shouts. Too loud. The couple at the table next to us look over and then look away.

Halmoni puts her hand on Mom's and forces her to set down the serving spoon. "We wait for spirits."

Mom's smile tightens. "Not here, all right? We're at a restaurant."

"You listen," Halmoni says to Mom. Then, to me, "Lily, you set table."

My palms sweat. It's really, really hot in here. "What do you mean?"

"We have to finish kosa. Where Andy? He come help us."

Sam chews on her fingernail. "Dad's not—" she starts, but Mom interrupts.

"He's at work. He'll be home soon," she says.

Halmoni looks around, but she's not really seeing. Her eyes shine like glass. She says something in Korean, something none of us can understand.

"Mom," I whisper. "What's happening?"

"Remember, we talked about this," Mom says quietly. "Sometimes Halmoni slips into the wrong place or the wrong time."

If Halmoni is seeing things that aren't there—if *she's* not *here*—then it's almost like she's not really Halmoni anymore.

She stands and walks over to the table next to us, singing a Korean lullaby as she picks up the man's plate. He sets his chopsticks on the table, making a startled sound.

Mom jumps up. "Mom, no, no. We don't need to do that." She takes the plate from Halmoni and returns it to the man, apologizing.

"It's okay," he says, sympathy in his eyes. "We know Ae-Cha. If there's anything we can do to help . . ."

But there's nothing they can do, because Halmoni moves around the table, taking the woman's plate and setting it on our table. "Danger is coming, so we make danger go 'way," she explains. "Kosa."

Only it's not kosa. It's consequences.

"Halmoni . . . ," Sam murmurs. Sam's always burying her fear, trying so hard not to be a QAG. But now she's afraid. Quiet.

Which makes everything worse.

Across the restaurant, a baby starts to cry, screaming its heart out. And I know I must have cried like that, but I can't imagine being so loud about my feelings, screaming when I needed to say, *My world is not right.*

"Mom," I whisper as Halmoni tries to take another plate. "We should go."

Aside from the baby, the whole restaurant is silent as people watch, pretending this isn't the worst moment of all time. Pretending this is okay.

Halmoni drops someone's plate, and it shatters on the floor, spilling soy-sauce-and-something-goo all over her shoes. One of the busboys runs over and tries to help, but nobody really knows what to do.

And then Mom—Mom who is so good at acting normal, who is always fake smiling—is grabbing Sam and me, and shoving Halmoni out the door, herding all of us, saying, "Go-go-go," all while Halmoni shouts about spirits and kosa and danger, and the gold cat statue waves *Goodbye! Goodbye!* and Sam keeps her head down, and I try to ignore that sweaty-hot-flashing-fainting feeling.

Then we're outside.

In the parking lot, Mom fumbles with the car door handle before thunking her head against the window. "I forgot my purse inside," she murmurs. "Will you girls get it? And leave a couple of twenties on the table for the bill."

Sam stays right where she is, but I nod.

I swallow and walk back into that restaurant, because I have to. Even though it's a too-hot bad place, and everyone is staring, and I don't want to.

I keep my head down as I fast-walk past the diners, grab Mom's purse, and throw money onto the table.

I pass the tiger painting, and I'm almost out the door when the waitress shouts, "Wait! Excuse me! Sorry! Wait!"

She runs up behind me, and I don't want to cry but my throat feels very swollen, like I might.

I don't know if I paid enough, or if she's mad about the food Halmoni dropped, or if she wants to ban me from the restaurant forever.

"Here's your food," she says, holding out a bag of take-out containers with our sweet-and-sour dishes inside.

I murmur a thank-you, and she holds out her other hand, shoving something into my palm. It's a pile of hard candies, the fruit ones that they give away at restaurants.

"Oh," I say, staring at them. I feel everyone very carefully *not* looking at us. Very intentionally *not* listening. "Okay."

"It's not enough," she says softly, "but my grandpa had Alzheimer's. And I know how hard it is. He was always forgetting where he was, and who we were, and . . . I'm just really sorry it's happening to you."

I want to tell her this isn't the same thing. Because

Halmoni would never forget us. This is just a side effect of releasing the star story, but she's going to get better, so it's not like the waitress's grandpa.

But it's still nice, that this girl cares. "Thanks," I say, and I hold the candies against my chest until it hurts a little less.

24

"Thanks for your help, girls," Mom says as we drive home from the restaurant.

Sam sits in the passenger seat, and Halmoni sits in the back with me, sleeping with her head on my shoulder.

I stay very still so I don't wake her.

Mom takes a breath. "At Halmoni's last doctor's appointment, the prognosis wasn't good. She could have a couple of months, or maybe just a week. But that's why I want to make the most of the good days. We just don't know."

Mom's words hang in the air for a few seconds, sucking up the oxygen.

And then Sam explodes. "Are you *kidding* me? This is so unfair. We come all this way and now she's just gonna die?"

Halmoni stirs next to me but doesn't wake. "Sam, quiet," I say. But my words feel flat. I can't think straight.

"We're here to spend time with her," Mom says. "To make the most of what we have."

"What if there's another way?" I ask, careful to keep my voice low. "What if there's something we can do?"

Of course Mom doesn't understand what I mean. "There are a few treatments," she explains, "but they have so many side effects, and it's never a sure thing. Halmoni isn't interested in that."

Side effects. Consequences. Why does hope always come at a price?

Sam says, "Well, it's worth it if she can live longer. Can't you just *make* her do them?"

Mom grips the steering wheel tighter. "We have to respect Halmoni. This is her choice, not ours."

"Yeah, but if there's something we can do and you're not doing it, you're basically *killing* her."

Sam's words slice through me, but I don't make any noise.

Mom says, "It's not like that."

Sam scoffs in disagreement.

"It's in God's hands now," Mom says, even though her words tilt up at the end, as if it's a question.

Outside, the world goes green, gray, green, gray, and I look for the tiger, but she's not there.

For once, Sam's words are soft. "What if I don't believe in God?"

Silence rings in my ears, and then Mom says something that moms are never supposed to say. "I don't know."

I scoot closer to Halmoni and curl my fingers into hers. She's fast asleep, but I imagine she's tracing my life line with her thumb. I imagine she's saying, *Everything is not fine, but it will be.*

Because I'll make it be. Mom doesn't see any other way. Sam doesn't believe in anything.

But I do.

And if they can't help Halmoni, I will.

After we get home, after we guide Halmoni up the outdoor steps and into her room, after Sam disappears into her headphones and cell phone, I tell Mom, "I need to make rice cakes."

Mom runs her hand over my hair and kisses my forehead. "Not today, honey. I'm sorry. Maybe tomorrow."

I shake my head. "It has to be today. I can't wait. I *have to.*"

Mom steps back, unsure what to do about my sudden fierceness. "Tomorrow, all right? I promise. I just don't want to do anything noisy or distracting for Halmoni. We need to keep the house quiet today, and we can't do anything that might upset her."

I don't understand how making rice cakes would upset Halmoni, but Mom won't budge.

So when she checks on Halmoni, I call Ricky.

"Hey," I say when he answers. "Can I come over?"

25

It's not hard to convince Mom.

As soon as I tell her I want to go to a friend's house, she agrees to drive me over that evening. Anything to get me out of the house. Anything to distract us.

After confirming with Ricky's dad, she says, "I'm so glad you're connecting with your peers." Which is an over-the-top way of saying *I'm glad you have friends* and is also the most Mom sentence of all time.

As we get closer to Ricky's, the shape of the town starts to change. The houses get bigger and the paint fresher. This side of town seems to expand—like Halmoni's side was a shrunken-down, forgotten version.

"Ricky Everett," Mom murmurs, double-checking the address on her phone. "I know his family."

"You know his dad?" I wonder if he was always scary

or if he just got that way when he grew up, but I'm not sure how to ask that.

"Sort of. His dad's a few years younger than me, so we went to high school at the same time but we weren't really friends. His family owns the paper mill, though, where most of the business in town is. So everyone knew *of* them."

I know it shouldn't matter, but it still takes me a second to adjust: Ricky's rich. I'm not sure how that changes my perception of him, but I feel like it does, just a little bit.

Our car putters into the long driveway, past bushes shaped like rabbits and cats. I've never seen anything like that, and I'm fascinated. They reshaped nature, just because they wanted to.

"This is . . . a lot," Mom murmurs. "Isn't it?"

I nod, gazing up at the house that is more of a mansion. There are two spiral stone columns framing the front door, and the big windows are covered with dark velvet curtains.

If Halmoni's house is a witch at the top of the hill, this house is a stuffy lady who works in a fancy museum and says *Shush* and *Don't touch* and *Step back.*

I can't picture Ricky in this house at all.

Mom parks and then grabs my hand before I can get out. "Call me as soon as you're ready to come home. If you're feeling upset or anything. I don't want you to feel guilty for being happy, but I don't want you to feel like you *have* to be happy, either."

My throat gets tight, so I just nod. We walk up to the front door and ring the doorbell. Instead of chiming, this doorbell starts playing classical music.

"I didn't know they could do that," I whisper to Mom.

She fights back a smile. "I think it's Bach."

Ricky's dad answers the door. He's wearing a button-down shirt and khakis, looking very put together for a Friday evening.

I just want to stare at my shoes and disappear, because I am Grocery Store Girl, but I force myself to be brave. I look up at him.

He smiles. He doesn't seem like a bad person, but maybe he's in disguise. "You must be Lily. It's nice to officially meet you. I'm Rick."

I blink. I know a lot of dads name their sons after themselves, but I still find it strange.

Mom nudges me and I clear my throat. "Nice to meet you," I say in my extra-polite voice.

"And Joan Ku!" He opens the door wider, inviting us in. "Long time no see!"

"It's Reeves now," Mom says. She grimace-smiles and hunches her shoulders, which is weird for her. Here she seems small.

We step inside, and—no surprise—the living room is

just as grand as the outside of the house. Its theme seems to be red, because there are red throw pillows on the red couch, red velvet curtains, and a red Oriental rug.

"You have a beautiful home," Mom says, her voice stilted and overly formal.

Ricky's dad shrugs, almost embarrassed. "My grandparents built the place."

I suck in a breath, because the house just got way more interesting. "The same ones who—" I remember too late that Ricky wasn't supposed to tell people about the tiger hunting, so I swallow my words. "Are Ricky's great-grandparents . . . ?" I finish, awkwardly. Now I *really* want to disappear.

He gives me a weird look, but it's not an unkind one. More of the classic *Kids?* look that adults seem to love.

Mom rubs my back, probably assuming I'm shaken up after what happened at lunch. I guess she's not wrong.

Ricky walks into the room wearing a black beanie with cat ears. "Lily! Come on!" he says, gesturing for me to follow.

"Remember to call me when you're done!" Mom says, holding her arm out like she wants to grab on to me and hang on forever.

I give her a little wave and leave the parents as they make small talk about *How long have you been in town?* and *Just moved back, looking for work.*

I want to take in the bigness of the house, but Ricky fast-walks through it, leading me out of the living room and past a series of . . . other living rooms.

There's a living room with a flat-screen TV, a living room with a pool table, a blue living room, and a yellow one. I try to peek into each one, secretly searching for evidence of tiger hunting, but I find nothing except for fancy art and furniture.

"Sorry about the house," Ricky says.

"Don't apologize. It's nice," I say, "like a museum."

He makes a face, and I feel bad. I remember what he said about my house, and I don't want to offend him.

Now I'm not sure if he was surprised by the strangeness of my home or the coziness of it. Halmoni's house feels safe and warm—Ricky's feels like you'll get yelled at for making a mess.

"Sorry. Never mind," I say as he leads me into the kitchen.

"It's cool that you're getting so into this," he says. "Are you gonna help with the poster making tomorrow, too?"

I stare at him. "What?"

"For the bake sale," he explains. "Isn't that why we're making these cakes?"

"Um." I open and close my mouth. I told him I needed to bake something, so of course that's the conclusion he drew. "Right! Yep. That is . . . yes."

He laughs. "You're strange."

"Oh."

"But not in a bad way." He clears his throat and looks like he's not sure what to say. "In an interesting way."

"Thanks," I say, though I'm not sure that's the right response. Sam always says *interesting* like *in-ter-es-ting,* in a way that clearly means *bad.* But when Ricky says it, it doesn't seem bad. It seems true.

I talk to tigers. I build magical traps. Maybe I *am* interesting.

He throws open a pantry that is bigger than our bathroom. Everything is color-coded and labeled. "I'm not really sure what's in here," he says. "Our chef uses all this stuff, and I don't spend much time in the kitchen."

I try not to show my surprise when he says *our chef,* but it's weird. "I don't know how to make rice cakes," I say, realizing only now how unprepared I am.

Ricky grins. "I don't know how to make *anything*!"

I Google a recipe on my phone, and we start throwing stuff together—mochi flour and brown sugar and coconut milk. Only somehow, the batter looks wrong. It's too lumpy and too runny at the same time, and it doesn't smell like Halmoni's.

On top of that, Ricky doesn't have adzuki bean paste for the filling, so we improvise with grape jelly, and by the time the rice cakes are ready to go into the oven, they look completely and totally wrong.

Which makes *me* feel completely and totally wrong.

And then I get that too-hot feeling again and my throat closes up and—"We have to throw these out. They're bad," I blurt.

Ricky frowns. "But . . . I want . . . to eat them?"

I lift the tray and spin around the kitchen, looking for the trash can. "Sorry, no. We can't. These have to be perfect. And they *aren't* perfect. They aren't like Halmoni's, because Halmoni can't make them right now, and I can't. I just can't."

"Okay, then," Ricky says. He takes the tray out of my hands, slowly, like you might approach a wild animal.

I stare at the tray. He stares at me.

"Are you okay?" he asks.

Still staring at the tray, I tell him, "My halmoni was acting weird. I don't know."

"Oh."

"Yeah."

He's quiet, because I think he knows: Sometimes, with the hard things, you don't want to talk about it. You just want someone to know it's happening.

After a maybe-too-long silence, he says, "My mom never used a recipe when she cooked. It turned out different every time. So we can still try these, if you want. Even if things aren't perfect, they can still be good."

I take a breath. And nod.

As the rice cakes bake, he distracts me by naming his top-twenty favorite foods, ranked (vanilla and chocolate pudding each have their own spot), until I blurt, "You should study harder for the language arts test."

I don't realize how mean that sounds until I see his face fall, but that's not how I meant it. "Because I know you can pass it," I explain. "You seem really smart. And you're going into seventh grade, right? So if you pass it, we'll be in the same grade. And we can be in middle school together."

As I say it, it strikes me how much I want that.

He looks up. "If we were in the same class, we could hang out a lot, and build *so many* tiger traps together."

"Well, maybe not tiger traps, but . . . other stuff."

He pauses, then asks, with hope sprawled across his face, "You really think I seem smart?"

I nod, embarrassed again. "I mean, yeah. You memorized your top-twenty favorite foods, and you helped me build a tiger trap, and you were right about the rice cakes being fine."

He grins, then tilts his head. "Well, let's wait and see about the rice cakes."

So we wait and see. And they're different. They aren't Halmoni's.

But they're still good.

Good enough, I hope, for a tiger.

26

I slam my phone alarm off as soon as it beeps me awake, and I slip out of bed, eager to meet with the tiger. I grab the tall, thin jar and the plate of rice cakes from under my bed and pad over to the stairs—but a rustling in the corner of the room stops me.

I spin around to see Sam fiddling with something by the window. "Did your alarm just go off at two a.m.?" she asks. She didn't say anything to me when I got back from Ricky's. She hasn't really spoken at all since the horrible lunch.

"No," I lie.

"Okaaay," she says before going back to her fiddling. I can tell she's still upset with me, though I don't know why. None of this is my fault.

I pause, waiting for her to interrogate me further, but

she doesn't. She's too busy with her own thing. I set down the plate and the jar. "What are you doing?" I ask.

She turns away from me. "Nothing." There's something weird in her voice, something wobbly and uncertain.

I walk over to her, and when I'm close enough, I realize she's tying a rope to her bed frame.

And not just any rope—but the rope Ricky and I used on the tiger trap. "Where did you get that?" I try to tug the rope out of her hands, but she yanks it from my grip. The rope burns my palms, and I rub them against my pajama pants.

"You left it by my bed," she says. "I figured you were done with it."

"I didn't . . ." Ricky and I tied the rope around the boxes for the tiger trap. But now that I'm thinking about it, I don't remember seeing the rope when I saw the tiger last night, just the boxes.

Sam shrugs and throws the rope out the window. It pulls taut against the bed frame, and I lean out the window. The rope dangles, nearly touching the ground. "Seriously? What are you doing?" I ask.

Sam glares at me. "Be quiet."

"What are you doing?" I whisper.

Sam shrugs. "I'm sneaking out," she says, like, *obviously.* "This house is suffocating."

I stare at her. "You're running away?" Halmoni ran

away from Korea. Mom ran away from Halmoni. And now Sam's running away from all of us. Maybe she can't help it. Maybe leaving runs in our genes. Maybe that's our family's superpower.

"No, Lily. Of course not. I'll be home before morning." Sam grabs her backpack and hoists herself up so she's sitting on the windowsill, her back to the open air. Watching her makes my stomach twist—if she leaned back, she'd tumble out the window.

I feel a tug in my chest now. The tiger is downstairs, I can tell. She's waiting. She's impatient. She's hungry.

But I don't want to leave Sam, and I don't want Sam to leave me. "Where are you going?" I ask.

"Where are *you* going?" she shoots back. "I saw you sneaking downstairs."

We stare at each other, both wanting to know, but neither wanting to give up our secrets.

She shakes her head. "Let's just agree not to tell Mom."

I hesitate. "Promise you'll be okay?"

"I'll be fine. I'll be back before morning." Her eyes soften. "And you, too?"

I extend my pinky. A pinky promise.

Long, long ago, a little sister cried. I'm afraid of the dark, *she said.*

So the older sister told her, I will be the moon. I will protect you, and you will never be afraid again.

Sam wraps her little finger around mine and we both squeeze. Then she grabs the rope and climbs out of the window, descending into the unknown—and I take the stairs.

Long, long ago, a tiger chased two sisters across the world. And just when they reached the end, just as the tiger leapt to swallow them, a magic rope fell from one end of the sky, and a magic staircase from the other.

In the story, the sisters always climb up, to safety. They aren't supposed to climb *down*. What happens when they climb back to earth—not together, but apart? When they realize there are tigers waiting at the bottom?

27

The tiger paces, muscles rippling as she circles the trap that could not contain her. She seems bigger tonight. As she passes through the narrow stream of light from the window, her fur seems to glow, like the moon is setting her stripes on fire.

I suck in a breath when I see her, but I find I'm not so afraid anymore.

"Haven't you heard?" She thunks down onto her hind legs, sitting, when I reach the bottom of the stairs. "Never keep a tiger waiting."

"Sorry," I say, then mentally tsk myself. I shouldn't apologize to her. I need to regain some power.

She makes a sound that is strangely close to one of Halmoni's tuts. "Now, where are my rice cakes?"

"Say *please.*" I try to sound confident and commanding, but she gives me a look as sharp as her teeth.

"Never mind," I mumble, holding out the plate.

She swallows the cakes whole, licking her lips and tilting her head. "Weird," she says. "Not how I'd make them. But acceptable. Story now."

I exhale and do as she says—uncorking the star jar and spilling the sky.

Long, long ago, when man roared like tiger, ten thousand days and ten thousand nights after a shape-shifter climbed into the sky and created the stars—a young girl lived with her halmoni in a little cottage by the sea. They lived alone, just the two of them, and they led a quiet life.

Every evening, the halmoni would try to tell the girl the story of their family. But the girl was afraid. The stories felt like darkness, the kind that hid under her bed and lurked beneath the stairs. No, Halmoni, *she said.* Tell me later. Sing to me instead.

Sighing, the halmoni would put the stories away and sing.

Goodnight stars,
goodnight air,
goodnight noises—

While she sang, the granddaughter would brew a cup of night-tea and stare up at the sky. Sometimes when the granddaughter looked at those stars, she felt like they'd been hung just for her—though she couldn't quite explain why.

As the tea steeped, the girl longed for the stars and fiddled with her pendant, an heirloom left behind by a mother she never knew.

One night, as the granddaughter poured the tea, the cup slipped from her hand. It cracked, spilling liquid amber across the table. Halmoni, I don't feel well.

Come closer, *Halmoni said.*

So the granddaughter came closer, leaning over the table, and Halmoni grabbed the girl's wrist.

It was much hotter than usual. And though the girl's skin looked as it always did, it felt coarse, like matted fur.

Aii-yah, it's too late. I should have told you sooner, the stories you need to know.

The granddaughter twisted, trying to escape, and when she did, her black hair caught in the moonlight, which lit up a stripe of bright white.

The girl was transforming before her halmoni's eyes—half human, half tiger.

Dark magic. Her granddaughter was cursed, the same way her daughter had been cursed.

Fight it, *Halmoni said.*

But the girl could not. Still she transformed.

She felt trapped in her own skin. She needed to escape. Her tiger heart turned angry. A wild thing, she rolled her terrible eyes and gnashed her terrible teeth.

The sea called to her tiger side, and she wanted so badly to taste freedom and salt on her tongue—to stare into an infinite horizon, to steal the stars, to swallow the world.

Somewhere in her heart, the girl knew: This was her mother's magic. Her mother would understand the wilderness she had become.

Halmoni didn't know what to do. She kept her granddaughter locked away.

But nothing worked.

So one night, the tiger-girl ran away, tracking the scent of her mother's stories.

She ran to the sea, and the sea parted just for her, and she crossed the ocean, crossed the world.

The sea collapsed again before Halmoni could follow, and Halmoni's heart broke. Partly because her granddaughter was gone. Partly because she couldn't help her.

But mostly because she worried: What if her granddaughter never knew how much her halmoni loved her?

Yes, her heart was broken, but she wouldn't give up.

She still loved the girl. She still wanted her to come home. Tiger or not.

So every full moon, she took a storage jar from her shelf

and whispered her heart into it. She filled the jars with love. A new kind of magic.

She didn't know where the girl had gone, but every full moon, she sent a jar into the sea, hoping the ocean would carry it off across the world.

She sent one month after month, until she was out of jars. But still, somehow, she hadn't run out of hope. Hope is a funny, lasting thing.

Halmoni believed that, somehow, her love would find her granddaughter.

And her granddaughter would find the way home.

When the story ends, I ask, "So if the girl had that pendant, was she the tiger-girl's daughter, from the first story?"

The tiger stares out the small window. In the light, she looks faraway and almost sad, but when she turns back to me, her eyes are fierce with shadows. "Perhaps. It seems that way."

"But if that's the case, she shouldn't have been cursed! The sky god said he would cure her. He lied!" I feel betrayed. Stories are supposed to have happy endings.

She sighs. "Unfortunately, sky gods are not so reliable. Maybe he had a different idea of *cured*. Maybe he made a mistake. Or maybe he was not as powerful as he claimed to be—maybe he couldn't control her heart."

I stare at the tiger. "But what happened to the granddaughter in the end?"

The tiger lowers her head. "She left."

"Did she ever find her way home?"

When the big cat speaks, there's a sharpness in her words. "This story is over."

"But the halmoni could have tried harder, right? They could have figured out how to cure her tiger curse and make everything better."

A growl rolls through the tiger's body. "Tiger blood is not the problem. Do you still think that?"

"Of course I do." I think about Sam climbing out the window, and I wonder if one day, I'll run, too. I wonder if that wildness lives in me—and I think it might. I feel it sometimes, bubbling inside, and I'm mad at the story for seeing that. "Tiger blood made her too wild, so she ran away from her halmoni, and then both of them were sad. What kind of story is that?"

"It's a dangerous one."

Her words pound between my ears. "How is this story going to cure my halmoni?"

"A cure is not about what we want. It's about what we need. The same is true for stories."

I have this strange feeling of fullness, like I'm going to burst. I'm going to explode. But all I say is, "I need Halmoni to get better."

I can't read the tiger's expression. It's almost tender, almost angry—and something else, too. "I will see you tomorrow. And don't bother bringing those unfortunate rice cakes."

She steps closer, so I can feel her breath on my skin—smell it, like dried squid and a hint of grape jelly. "Bring me the final star jar. And don't be late. You are running out of time."

28

The living room is quiet except for the ticking grandfather clock. I tiptoe past Mom, careful to avoid the creaky floorboards.

I carry the jar in one hand and the empty rice cakes plate in the other. When I reach the kitchen sink, I place the plate inside. Careful, careful, quiet.

It clinks as I set it down, and I hold my breath, but Mom doesn't wake. I should go back upstairs as soon as I can, but I take a moment, holding the star jar up to the window.

The jar feels different now. Not as heavy. And it's like the glass collects moonlight, gathering it all and beaming it right into me.

"Lily?"

I nearly drop the jar as I spin around to see Mom lying

on the couch, rubbing sleep from her eyes. "What are you doing up?" she asks.

"I was just . . . hungry." My hands shake, and I set the jar on the counter.

I wait for her to ask me about the jar, to tell me how late it is, to explain the importance of a regular sleep schedule in times of emotional stress. But she yawns and stands.

She slides her glasses on, cracks her back, walks right past the star jar, and throws the refrigerator door open. "What do you want to eat?"

"Um," I say.

Mom scans the food as she blinks herself awake, and pulls out Halmoni's plastic tub of kimchi. "Sound good?" she asks, holding it up.

I nod, not trusting myself to say anything. I glance over at the jar, but Mom's too tired to notice.

She pushes herself up so she's sitting on the counter and motions for me to join her.

I hesitate because this is *not* typical Mom behavior. But I hop up next to her, even though I'm partially waiting for her to scold me.

Mom just unscrews the lid and fishes out a piece of kimchi with her fingers. Then she drops the piece right into her mouth and smacks her lips.

When she holds the tub out to me, I stare at my mother. Any moment now, she'll wake up and realize she was sleepwalking. And sleep-eating. And sleep-rule-breaking.

Mom laughs. "Lily. Stop looking at me like I have three heads."

"It's just . . ."

She pushes the kimchi tub closer. "Eat."

So I take a piece of kimchi and chew it, letting the spicy-sour-salty flavor settle my stomach.

Maybe nothing is too weird in the middle of the night. Spirits might slip into these moments, between waking and dreaming—but love does, too.

Mom wraps her arm around me, pulling me closer. "I'm sorry, Lily," she whispers, into my ear. "I'd hold back the world if I could. I'd take away all your pain. But you've already faced such hard things. I'm sorry I couldn't protect you."

I bite my cheek. Even though it's not fair, I want to ask: *Why couldn't you?*

But I think about the tiger-girl, how she left her baby behind to protect her. I think about the halmoni who told her granddaughter to hide and fight.

Those protections didn't work. In the end, they only made things worse.

When Mom looks at me, her eyebrows lift a little, like she's seeing something surprising—something new.

She's about to speak, but something catches her attention. "Where'd you find that jar?"

My heart stutters. "Um . . . just in Halmoni's old stuff."

"Huh. It looks familiar." Mom frowns, just slightly. I catch a hint of recognition on her face, but it flits away. "Ah, I'm sure I just saw it around when I was a kid."

She slides off the counter and screws the lid back onto the kimchi. "Get some sleep," she tells me, voice soft. "Things are always easier in the morning."

29

I wake up late the next day, catching up on all the sleep I lost to the tiger. Sam's not here, but the window is closed and the rope is rolled up under her bed, so that's a good sign.

I get dressed and braid my hair, checking on the star jars under my bed. I carried the tall one up last night, and now they're all together again, cuddled in a row like a little family.

I head down the stairs, but after a few steps, something sharp digs into my bare feet. I lift my foot and realize it's *rice*—uncooked grains, scattered across the steps. Which is weird.

I brush them off, but I don't have much time to think about it, because when I go downstairs, I see that Halmoni has cooked enough Korean food to fill the entire kitchen.

Sam helps Halmoni, humming to herself as she carries the finished dishes to the table, and seeing my sister fills me with relief. She sets mandoo on the table, and I almost see her smile. But just as quickly her happiness fades, and she shakes her head.

I wish I knew what she was thinking. If I did, maybe I could reach out and catch Sam's smile before it falls to the floor and shatters.

Mom cleans the kitchen, because that's what she always does, but even she seems happy, swaying back and forth to the music playing on Sam's phone—one of the songs only Sam likes, with string instruments playing rock covers.

Halmoni looks happy and healthy, wearing a pink-and-purple scarf over her hair and smiling as she seasons the naengmyeon, my favorite noodles. When Halmoni cooks, the house seems to expand, like it's taking a deep breath, savoring the smell of her food.

The ceiling seems higher, the walls seem wider, and the floorboards rumble like an empty stomach as I walk into the kitchen to join her.

"Are you doing a kosa?" I ask.

Sam shakes her head. "Nope. We're just eating lunch, on our own. The spirits can deal with it."

Halmoni smiles at me. "You hungry?" she asks. Without waiting for an answer, she picks up a piece of kimchi with two fingers and holds it out to me. "Eat fast so spirits don't see," she whispers.

In that moment, she's so much like Mom that I glance over at the kitchen sink, where Mom's polishing a dish. Mom must see the similarity, too, because she winks.

I'm all filled up, because last night is like our secret. And that's nice, because Mom and I never share secrets.

I eat the kimchi, and Mom says, "I've been waiting for you to wake up, Lily. I actually spoke to Ricky's dad this morning, and—"

"Now you, Joanie," Halmoni interrupts, grabbing a piece of kalbi and attempting to stuff the beef into Mom's mouth.

Mom protests, ducking her head away from the meat, but Halmoni insists, trying to shove it into her mouth.

"This is ridiculous," Mom says. She runs to the other side of the living room, so startled that she laughs.

Halmoni chases her, moving surprisingly fast. Kalbi dangles from her fingertips. "You eat! You eat!"

I look over at Sam, who's grinning despite herself. "They're making enough noise to attract all the spirits in the neighborhood," she says, and I laugh.

Finally, Mom gives up and opens her mouth. "Goodness, Mother," she says, her mouth full of kalbi.

"You listen," Halmoni says to Mom. "The spirits say you need rest. You need to stop worry."

Mom's eyebrows pinch. Not a storm cloud yet, but a shift in the air. "You know why I'm worrying so much."

Halmoni raises her hands in defense. "Not *me* that say that. *Spirits* say that."

When Mom rolls her eyes, Sam and I look at each other. Sam tilts her head toward the attic room. *Let's go,* she mouths.

But I don't want to go. I want to stay here and bring the happy moment back.

"Halmoni," I say, trying to distract her, "what else should we do to prep the food?"

Halmoni turns and shuffles across the room, grabs me by the wrists. "Lily, the spirits keep telling you to be careful. *'Be safe! Be safe!'* They say that to me."

I swallow and lie, "I am." Beside me, I feel Sam stare, but I don't look at her.

Halmoni leans closer, and her eyes fall to my neck, to the pendant hovering right above my heart. "Where you get that?"

I try to pull away, but she holds my wrists hard. "What do you mean? You gave it to me."

"No, that mine. Someone give me that, long, long ago. I remember." She shakes her head. "But I don't give you that. Why you saying that?"

I don't know how to respond, but Sam interrupts. "Halmoni, you did. Remember?"

Halmoni turns and walks to Sam. When she reaches my sister, Halmoni runs her fingers over Sam's white streak. "This like me, when I back at home. So long ago. So long, I try to forget."

My limbs go cold. The pendant. The white streak. They were both in the star stories.

So this is another consequence. And how many more consequences can I handle? How many can Halmoni handle?

Mom steps in, pulling Halmoni away from Sam. "Don't scare them," she whispers. "We should eat now."

Halmoni looks back and forth between Sam and me, confused. Her eyes don't adjust properly. It's like she's seeing a different world.

But when Halmoni looks into my eyes, she recoils. "A tiger," she hisses.

I step back. "What? No. Halmoni. It's *me.*"

My heart roars in my ears. The whole world is upside down. I want to run from her.

Halmoni sways a bit—dizzy. Unsteady.

I wait for her to recognize me. To see me. I am her little egg. Her Lily Bean.

But she frowns. "You are . . ."

I wait for her to finish—I wait and wait—but she doesn't.

And I realize: she can't remember.

And it's not just that, but there's something worse, too—a flash of panic behind her eyes. It's not that she can't remember my name. It's that she can't remember *me.*

She doesn't know me.

She doesn't *see* me.

There's a bottom-out feeling in my stomach, because she's a stranger in Halmoni's skin.

Who is Halmoni without her memories?

And who am *I* without Halmoni?

Voice cracking, I whisper, "It's me. Lily Bean."

Halmoni smiles a plastic Mom-fake-smile. "Yes, my Lily Bean. I, uh, I go rest now." She kisses me on the forehead and I flinch.

"Come on, Mama," Mom says, guiding her back into her bedroom, shutting the door behind them. Locking us out.

"It's okay." Sam takes a shaky breath. "It's just temporary. She'll be back to normal soon."

I nod, but I can't make myself speak.

"The library!" Sam exclaims out of nowhere.

I blink at her, trying to make sense of the world.

"Jensen's making signs and stuff today." She grabs her raincoat and slips it on. "Let's go."

Right. Somewhere in my memory, I know Ricky mentioned that. But I'm not sure how Sam knows. "You actually want to do that?"

Sam looks confused, as if she *always* participates in community activities and doesn't understand my question. "Of course. Jensen and I have been—talking. And, yeah, you know. It's nice to help out." When her eyes meet mine, they are helpless. "And I don't want to be here right now."

Sam's out the door before I can respond, and I only have a split second to decide: Stay or follow?

I'm not in the mood to see people and act happy right now, but one glance at Halmoni's closed door makes up my mind.

I can't stay here anymore.

30

Sam and I reach the library, and when we open the doors, I hear music. And laughter.

The change of atmosphere is disorienting.

On one side of the library, Jensen crowds around her laptop with a girl and a boy who both look about her age, and on the other—Ricky sits with his back to me, at a table with two other boys. I'm overwhelmed and want to turn around immediately, but Joe stops me.

"Lily!" he shouts over the pop music, almost smiling.

I walk over to him and introduce Sam, who shakes his hand and smiles, as if nothing's wrong and our lives are totally fine.

Joe pulls a cupcake out from behind his desk and hands it to me. I take it, not quite knowing what to do.

"I'm making a tester batch," he says. His mustache

twitch-twitches above his smile. "Let me know what you think."

It's a nice gesture, but I don't think I can eat it. I'm too anxious right now. I feel like everyone can see *SICK GRANDMA* written on my forehead, and I don't want to face the world.

Jensen sees us and dances over, hips bop-popping to the music. "Sam!" Her smile is so big it makes double parentheses on her cheeks. "And Lily! I'm so glad you're here."

She looks at Sam for two heartbeats and says, "You any good with tech? We're setting up an *email newsletter* for the library and scaring Joe with all this newfangled technology."

Sam laughs, and if it weren't for the tension in her shoulders, I would think she forgot about what just happened.

Jensen pulls her away, and then I'm standing alone in front of Joe's desk.

This is why I didn't want Sam here. When she's here, there's no space for me. I can't stay home. I can't stay here. I am lost.

"Lily." Joe clears his throat, looking concerned and uncomfortable. "What's the matter?"

"Nothing. I should go," I say, even though I really don't want to go home.

Joe frowns. "Don't you want to see the noisy kid and his friends?"

I look over at Ricky and his group and shake my head.

Joe sighs, and then, as if he's already regretting it, he says, "You can talk to me."

I don't mean to, but it's like he's said a magic spell, and I do. "My halmoni used to tell us these stories, when I was little. And I really loved them. But now I'm learning these new stories, and they're different. They're scary. And I think they're . . . dangerous, because they're making things change in ways that I don't think are good. Actually, I think things are worse now, all because I decided to hear these new stories and . . ."

I realize I'm not making any sense, so I take a breath and add, "I just miss the way things used to be. I don't want anything to change."

I clamp my lips shut, horrified that I've said so much. But opening up is also a relief. I glance back at Sam and Jensen and Ricky and the rest—but they're busy, and they can't hear me over the music, anyway.

Joe nods slowly. "As you get older, you collect more information and you see things from different perspectives. So, naturally, sometimes the stories you tell yourself . . . can change."

I twist my hands together. "But what if those stories aren't what you want them to be?"

His eyes are soft. "Do you know why I became a librarian?"

I wait for him to tell me, because of course I don't.

"Dewey," he says. "As in the decimal system."

I'm not sure if he's joking or not, but he continues, "I like order. I like organization. The idea of all the information in the world, all organized, everything in its place—I like that idea."

He clears his throat. "But I've been doing this job for a long time. And the thing I've learned is that stories aren't about order and organization. They're about feelings. And feelings don't always make sense. See, stories are like . . ." He pauses, brow furrowing, then nods, satisfied in finding the right comparison: "Water. Like rain. We can hold them tight, but they always slip through our fingers."

I try to hide my shock. Joe doesn't seem like the *poetic* type.

His caterpillar eyebrows knit together. "That can be scary. But remember that water gives us life. It connects continents. It connects people. And in quiet moments, when the water's still, sometimes we can see our own reflection. Do you understand what I'm saying?"

"Kind of," I say, even though I'm not entirely sure.

Joe's eyes are almost shiny, and I wonder what's slipped through his fingers. I've just thought of him as Grouchy Librarian Man, but I realize now that I saw only a piece of him. His story is so much bigger. He's had this whole life, a life I might never know about.

"Thanks, Joe," I say.

He looks over my shoulder. "Well, the noisy kid is waving rather frantically."

Behind me, I hear Ricky's voice. "Lily!"

I turn to see Ricky with the other boys. "Hello!" he says, grinning. "These are my friends, and now they're your friends, too."

He introduces them—Connor, a pale boy with green plastic glasses, and Adam, a freckly kid with curly red hair.

The three of them *match* each other. All boys, same skin tone, same height, same burst-out-of-your-skin energy.

Adding me to this mix is like throwing a carrot into a bowl of fruit salad and hoping nobody notices the difference.

I try to act like a regular girl. I try not to go invisible. I try to pretend that everything is fine at home.

But I'm trying so hard that I forget to respond. "Hi," I mumble after a second, forcing a smile.

Connor and Adam stand around Ricky, with him at the center. Turns out I was right: Ricky is a sticky person.

"Oh, man! How'd you get one of Joe's cupcakes?" he asks.

I look down at my hand. I forgot I had it, and I hold it out for him to eat.

"You're the best," he says as he takes it and bites into it. "These are so good. But I'm still craving pudding."

Connor, with the glasses, snorts. "Pudding, Ricky? Really? Pudding is gross."

Ricky shakes his head, offended. "Chocolate pudding is the fourth most delicious food. Everyone knows that." He looks over at the teenager table. "I'm gonna ask Jensen if she has any pudding cups."

Adam, of the freckles, shakes his head. "Dude, chill." He turns to me and his eyes crinkle. He looks familiar, though I'm not sure why. "So, Lily, where are you from?"

My brain goes blank for a second. Then I say, "I'm from across the street."

For some reason, I feel like that wasn't the answer he was looking for, but he gives me half a nod—a quick jerk of his chin. "You mean the house on the hill? With that lady?"

"She's my grandma."

Connor's eyebrows go high. "The crazy witch lady is your *grandma*?"

I want to tell him, *Crazy is not a thinking word.* But my mouth feels dry.

Connor keeps talking, "That's so cool. I heard she, like, does spells and curses people. Did she teach you how? Can you put a curse on someone?"

I look to Ricky, waiting for him to defend Halmoni, to

defend *me.* But he just takes another bite of the cupcake and nods along.

Adam says, "Nah, she doesn't curse people. She cures them. My mom is convinced Lily's grandma healed her asthma. But my mom also believes in TV psychics, so who knows." And I realize why he seems so familiar—I met his mom at the grocery store. They have the same red hair and freckles. She's one of Halmoni's friends.

Connor is unconvinced. "I don't know. The witch lady is *scary.*"

I lift my fingers to my neck, searching for the pendant—but I drop it quickly. It's not safe anymore.

"I . . ." Guilt claws at my stomach. I should defend Halmoni, but all my words have evaporated.

And for a moment, I don't want to defend her. For a moment, I wish she were a normal grandmother, who makes brownies instead of kimchi. Who knits scarves instead of mixing strange Korean herbs.

Ricky finally speaks, mouth still full. "Guys, Lily's grandma's not scary. It's not her fault she's like that. She's sick, so she has hallucinations that make her act that way, like scared of ghosts and tigers and stuff, right, Lily?"

The ground becomes a black hole—a tiger's mouth, jaws open wide—and I'm falling in, swallowed whole.

He wasn't supposed to tell.

But that's not even the worst part.

The worst part is that when I heard Ricky say that, it felt like the sickness is all that Halmoni is. Like the sickness is the *reason* for how she is.

But Halmoni isn't like that because she's sick. She's like that because she's *Halmoni.* Because she's magic. She's always been that way.

Now it feels like there's something *wrong* with that.

Halmoni buys rice and pine nuts and herbs to cast magic, she feeds spirits, she believes in all the things you cannot see. She lives in a house at the top of a hill, a house covered in vines, with windows that watch like unblinking eyes.

She is a witch, looming over the town, like something out of a fairy tale.

She's not normal.

I'm not normal.

And I thought Ricky was on my side, but he's not. He's horrible, like those horrible other boys, and I was wrong to think we could ever be friends.

I feel like there's a spotlight on me, and my eyes start to burn. I look at the floor, begging myself not to cry.

Connor looks uncomfortable, eyes darting between Ricky and me. "Pudding!" he blurts. "Ricky, maybe you should ask Jensen for pudding—now."

"I'll get it," I say, grateful for the escape.

I walk away fast. Ricky calls after me, but I need to get

away from them. I walk down the hallway, past Jensen and Sam and the other teenagers, past rows of books, into the staff room at the back of the library.

It's quiet back here, and the silence sounds like relief. The cat poster tells me to hang in there.

I take a deep breath and open the refrigerator to take out a chocolate pudding.

And then I stop.

This is ridiculous. Ricky was mean to me, and I didn't stand up for Halmoni or myself, and now I'm *fetching him a pudding.*

That's pathetic. That's classic QAG behavior.

But a thought pops into my head—uninvited. It's not a thought that should belong to me. It's like it comes from somewhere else entirely. But as I stand there, staring at the pudding, that thought settles in my stomach, thick and heavy as mud.

31

Before I can second-guess myself, I grab the chocolate pudding, turn myself invisible, and slip out the back door of the staff room, into the rain.

The ground is soft and slimy and, if you think about it, looks a lot like pudding.

I pull the foil lid off the cup, carefully and only slightly, so you couldn't tell the cup had been opened unless you were looking really hard. Then I dump some of the pudding onto the ground and scoop mud inside.

Halmoni fed Dad mud because he spoke too much without thinking. And if Ricky wants a curse, he's going to get one. I hold my hands over the pudding cup and focus all my energy onto it, feeling ridiculous but also powerful.

I am not a weak, quiet girl. I will defend my halmoni. I am brave, and I believe.

I stare at the pudding and think, *Be nice, Ricky. Think before you speak.* Then I add, *And get a stomachache.* Just for good measure.

My heart screams wildly in my ears, and I half expect to be caught by Jensen or Joe, but nobody else is around. Nobody except—

I look up to see the tiger sitting in front of me, tail dancing in the rain.

"What are you doing here?" I ask, rubbing raindrops from my eyes.

"What, a tiger can't enjoy the library? It happens to be my favorite place."

I stare at her. "What do you want?"

She lifts one shoulder in a shrug, and her stripes ripple like waves. "I am merely observing. Just as you observe us in zoos."

I lower the pudding and let rain run into my mouth as I say, "Halmoni forgot about the pendant and Sam's white streak today."

"Was she forgetting or remembering?"

I glare at her, sick of riddles.

"You must reach the end—"

"And then *what*? And then Halmoni is cured? And then the stories stop being scary? Tell me what happens."

She doesn't respond.

"I'm sick of everyone hiding things from me. I'm sick

of people acting like I'm not there, or I don't matter, or I can't do anything."

The pudding trembles in my hands. "I'm not an invisible little girl. I'm not a QAG." I spin around and walk back toward the library door.

"I was wrong about you," the tiger says.

I stop, but I don't turn around. The back of my neck prickles.

"It seems you have a tiger side after all."

I spin to face her, and she sits, watching me as her tail flicks.

For a second, her words almost feel true. I feel fierce and strong. I feel unstoppable, like my teeth could turn to blades and my nails to claws. Like I could stand up for myself and nobody could ignore me.

But I'm not like her, because she's the villain and I'm the hero. I fix things, whether it's Ricky's rudeness or Halmoni's illness. I make things better, and I don't trick people, making them *wait for the end* while bad things happen.

"I'm not a monster," I tell her. "Leave me alone."

She tsks, a sharp sound that scrapes against her teeth. "As you wish."

And then, in a flash, she's gone. I am alone again, in the rain, with only the pudding cup clutched to my chest.

I shake her out of my head and slip back inside, then lean against the door, heart thudding.

I won't let her upset me. I won't second-guess this.

I wring out my hair, shake the droplets off my raincoat, and wipe my face with a paper towel. Then I take another towel to dry the pudding cup, and I smooth out the foil lid. I'm surprised at my handiwork. You can hardly tell I've messed with it.

I grab a plastic spoon from one of the drawers and head back to Ricky's group. With the tiger gone and the chocolate-mud pudding in hand, I feel much better than before.

"You're all wet!" Ricky announces when I give him the cup and spoon.

Adam frowns. "Are you okay?"

"I just wanted some air," I say.

Ricky doesn't hear the tension in my voice.

He trusts me.

He lifts the spoon, peels back the foil without noticing anything.

Too late, I question my decision. Maybe, at least, I shouldn't have added the stomachache part.

But I don't stop him. I stand there and watch as he takes a spoonful, lifts it to his lips, and swallows.

That moment stretches into infinity.

Then his nose crinkles. "Something's wrong with this pudding."

Adam says, "Don't eat it if it tastes weird."

"Wait," Ricky says. He takes another bite and nods in confirmation. "Yes, the pudding is weird."

I feel a little dizzy. I need to go, but I can't leave now without being obvious.

"I think there's something in it." Ricky takes another bite and shakes his head. "I'm not sure what—"

Connor grabs it from Ricky's hands and tastes it for himself. "Weird," he says. "Weird for sure."

Adam frowns at the cup. "If you think it's weird, don't eat it. The consistency looks off. It could be poop."

Ricky's eyes pop. "I ate *poop?!*"

Across the library, I see Jensen look over at us in confusion, and all the boys start talking about poop at once.

"It was just mud!" I blurt.

They go silent, staring at me. Panicked, I try to go invisible, but they won't stop staring.

"It was just mud," I say, quieter now. "Mud isn't that bad."

They blink in shock, and Ricky looks at me with a mixture of fear and awe. "You *cursed* me," he whispers.

And I can't deal anymore. I turn and run out of the library, sprinting across the street without looking both ways.

The library door slams behind me and I hear Sam calling my name, but I don't look back. I don't stop. I take the steps three at a time as I run up, up, up to the witch's house.

32

When I run into Halmoni's house—panting, wild—Mom's digging through the kitchen cupboards.

"Have you seen the rice?" she asks without turning around. "I could have sworn we had a big bag of it, but I can't find it. I need something to settle Halmoni's stomach—"

Sam bursts through the door behind me, panting, too, her eyes wide. "What did you *do*? Like, seriously?! You totally embarrassed me!"

"Embarrassed *you*? Stop making everything about you!"

Mom turns around and fixes her red-rimmed eyes on us. I realize she's been crying. "All right," she says. "What's going on?"

Sam and I answer at the same time.

I say, "Nothing."

But Sam says, "Lily put *mud* in that kid's *pudding.*"

"Sam!" I hiss as the betrayal whips through me. *Sisters keep secrets. Sisters keep each other's secrets.*

Mom waits for more information, but neither of us speaks. "Excuse me?" Mom asks finally.

Sam looks at me and bites her lip. "Sorry, it just came out—" she starts to say, but Mom cuts her off.

"Lily, what is Sam talking about? What kid?"

I glare at Sam, wishing she could suck the words back into her chest and cork them tight.

But they're out there, and I can't do anything about it. "Ricky," I mumble.

Mom pauses. Her face goes pale. "Sam," she says, her voice far too soft. "Halmoni's not feeling well. Why don't you take her some of your nut crackers? Lily and I need a moment alone."

Sam tries to catch my eye, but I won't look at her. She grabs her crackers and disappears into Halmoni's room.

She leaves me with Mom. And Mom is furious.

It's not like I haven't seen Angry Mom before, but she's always angry at Sam. *I'm* never the problem. It's never *me.*

"What were you *thinking*?" she asks. "What possessed you to do that?"

I don't answer. Where would I even begin?

"Nope, nope. Never mind. I know *exactly* where that mud idea came from. Don't think I don't realize. Oh my god, how did I fail *this badly*?"

I hate how everyone is making this about them. I'm the one who did it, and they're just erasing me. "I saw something wrong, so I did something about it."

"Okay, Lily, but feeding your friend mud was *also very wrong*." Mom blows out a long stream of air. "I know things have been hard. But I'd never expect you to act out like that. This sounds like something *Sam* would do."

I want to tell her that maybe her idea of *Sam* and *Lily* isn't quite as clear as she thought. The story has always been that Sam acts out and I'm invisible.

But maybe Sam doesn't get to claim all the anger in the world. Maybe I don't *want* to be invisible.

"Lily, I understand you're upset. But this isn't you."

Only—it is.

I've changed. Maybe the star stories really have changed me, or maybe I've changed myself. Somehow, that's both thrilling and terrifying.

Mom rubs her hands over her face. "Ricky's dad just offered me a job. That's what I was going to tell you this morning."

I take a breath. "What?"

"His dad . . ." She sighs. "We were talking about how I'm looking for work, and he called to offer me an accounting position at Everett Mills. It's just . . . it was such a relief to get a job, and—well, that's not the point."

I feel bad now. But I didn't know. It's not my fault. And Ricky's dad won't fire Mom based on something *I* did.

"Regardless, you have to apologize to that boy. You know that, right?"

California Lily would have nodded and done what she was told. But I don't just follow orders anymore. Nobody tells me what to do. Not even tigers. "But, Mom, he was being mean about Halmoni! You didn't hear him. He and his friends called her a witch. They said she was crazy and scary. *That* was bad. *Mud* is not that bad."

Mom pulls me over to the kitchen table to sit with her. Her lips are still a white-tight, thin line. Her face and neck are still flushed. But some of the anger drains from her eyes. "Listen, Lily. I wasn't there, but I'm sure I know exactly what they were saying. I spent my *whole life* growing up with that. Halmoni is eccentric and strange, and not everybody understands her individuality."

I *skritch* my nails against the table. "Eccentric and strange aren't bad things."

She sighs. "I know that. You know that. But other people aren't always so kind. And it's hard—especially now. But Halmoni doesn't need you putting mud in people's pudding for her. She needs you to be there, to focus on her. And when you do something like this, you're spending more energy on the people who don't understand Halmoni than on Halmoni herself."

In the moment, I felt like I was doing the right thing. I was protecting Halmoni. But now Mom's making me feel like I did something wrong—like somehow doing that *hurt* Halmoni.

My stomach twists, as if I've eaten my own mud pudding. "Do you ever feel ashamed that she's your mom?" I whisper. The words come out quickly. My heart beats hard, almost as hard as it did when I talked to the tiger—as if asking a question is just as scary as facing a beast. "Did you ever get embarrassed by her, as a kid?"

"Oh." Mom goes soft. "Of course I did. I think everyone feels embarrassed by their family sometimes. But the embarrassment was never ever as strong as the pride I felt, because she's pretty incredible, isn't she?"

I nod, and then I remember something else Joe said, the first time we met. "Joe—the librarian—he said you and Halmoni were close." I scratch at the peeling purple paint on the table. "What happened?"

"Nothing bad, Lily. We're still close now." Then Mom corrects herself, because we both know that's a lie. "I still *love* her."

She tap-tap-taps her fingers against her knee. "Your halmoni worked a lot when I was little. When we moved here, she took on a lot of odd jobs. She'd find things that people needed help with, and she'd figure out how to do it.

"And I wanted to help her. It's how we spent time together. I was her little assistant, trailing after her, translating, writing everything in English."

I can't imagine Mom following Halmoni around like that. I can't really imagine her little at all, and I wonder what she used to be like—if she used to be a QAG, too. And if she was, I wonder how she changed that.

Mom says, "Halmoni made it work in a world that was stacked against her, but she was always so busy. She was a single mom, so she had to be. That was the hardest part, because sometimes she didn't have time for me."

I don't understand how Halmoni can be the only person who makes me feel seen, but can also make Mom feel so forgotten. How is that possible? How could one person do such opposite things at the same time?

"And then?" My voice cracks. I'm afraid of what comes next.

But Mom shakes her head. "There's nothing bad, Lily. Nothing magical or interesting, not like her fairy tales. It was just . . . real life. I grew up."

I don't want to be like that when I get older. I don't want to drift apart or away. I pull my legs up and curl my knees into my chest.

"Lily, my relationship with Halmoni never ended. It just changed."

"I don't want things to change," I say.

She looks at me intently, like she needs me to understand. "Lily, everything changes. That's normal. But I never stopped loving her. That's why we're here, because I love her so much. We all do. And I know Halmoni's episodes are scary, but she loves you, too. Those momentary lapses are the illness, not her."

I think about the mud, and a pit of shame grows in my stomach. "I let her down."

"I did, too," Mom says, so quietly that her words are almost lost to the sound of rain. "But we're trying our best, and that's what matters. We're all just trying our best."

33

Mom wants me to apologize, but she gives me time to reflect, so we decide: tomorrow.

Tonight: *Think about what you want to say.* Tonight: *Get some sleep. Rest.*

Which shouldn't be hard, because by the time night falls, I'm exhausted.

Sam is upstairs waiting.

She sits cross-legged on her bed, headphones suffocating her ears, and she rips them off as soon as she sees me. "I didn't mean to rat you out."

I walk past her and flop onto my bed.

"But you have to admit," she says, "that was wild. Why'd you *do* that?"

I close my eyes. I have to see the tiger later, but for now my bed is warm and cozy.

"Lily?" Sam insists, leaning forward in her bed. There's something almost panicked in her voice. "What's wrong with you? Answer me. I already said I was sorry. Why won't you answer me?"

I pretend I am Sam, with headphones jammed against my ears. I pretend I am Sam, staring at a glowing screen, ignoring the world around me. I pretend I am Sam and I do not answer.

If she can't be trusted with secrets, I won't tell her any.

I curl up in bed and pull the blankets over my head.

Long, long ago, when tiger walked like man, there were two sisters. . . .

Sam exhales sharply. "You're *really* gonna give me the silent treatment?"

The two sisters loved each other, more than anything. More than rice cakes. More than the earth. More than the stars.

"You know," she goes on, "it's not like mud would actually keep people grounded or anything. There's no *magic.* Like, really. We have to grow up. We can't keep believing in all these things."

Buried under the covers, I stare at the tiny holes in my quilt. They look like stars, and I make a wish on one of them. I wish that Sam would stop talking.

But she doesn't. Sam is on a roll, and she won't stop now, no matter how hard I wish.

She says, "You think this is all about you? You think

you're the only one who's upset? I hate this. I hate it here. I hate that we're watching Halmoni forget her life and forget us and we're watching her *die.*" The words spiral out of her fast. She takes a breath. "But whatever. I just want it to end. I want it to be *over* already."

Her words chill the room by ten thousand degrees.

My heart stammers, and I push the covers back. "Take it back," I say. "Knock on wood."

Her voice is ragged, broken glass. "I don't believe in that stuff anymore."

"But you have to. How could you say that?"

She doesn't answer. She swallows and looks almost doubtful, like she knows she's wrong.

But then she shrugs and turns away, disappearing into her blankets.

* * *

I lie in bed without moving, breathing hard, waiting for what feels like hours, until Sam falls asleep.

When she's snoring, when the coast is clear, I sneak downstairs to deliver the third star jar to the tiger. Sam might not believe, but I do.

I push the basement door open, but when I creak down the steps, I find only an empty room.

The tiger isn't there.

It's just a dusty basement with a bunch of old boxes, lit by a thin strip of window.

"Hello?" I whisper, but there's nothing. No trace of magic tonight.

The tiger said we were running out of time to help Halmoni, and now the tiger's gone, and I don't know why—but then I remember.

I told the tiger to leave me alone, and she said, *As you wish.*

Only I didn't mean *completely.* Now she's gone, and I don't know how to unwish it.

34

I wake up with worry weighing on my chest, heavy as a tiger.

I waited in the basement for almost an hour, but she never showed up, and I never felt that *pull* right below my heart—that unsettling sense of impatience that told me she was waiting.

If she's mad about what I said—if I wished her away and she won't come back to the basement—I have to find her somewhere else. I have to get her back and finish the stories before there's more consequences. Before the worst consequence.

I'm distracted for most of the morning, but after breakfast Mom tells me to get dressed. It's time to apologize.

"You'll feel better afterward," she tells me, and I know

she's probably right, but I still take forever to get ready, brushing my teeth for five minutes, braiding and rebraiding my hair.

It's not that I don't want to say I'm sorry. But it doesn't have to be *now.* I have other things to think about. Before I go downstairs, I break off a new piece of mugwort and stuff it into my pocket. It didn't do much to protect me from the tiger, but maybe it will protect me from awkward conversations.

Then I lift the camo top hat from my dresser. I have to return it.

I hold it in my hands and try to ignore the sadness inside me, the feeling that something has changed and I can never go back.

Mom packs me into the car and drives me to Ricky's.

"You've got to do it now, Lily," she says. "If you put things off for later, you'll never do them. They'll become harder and scarier, and one day you'll realize you've run out of time."

I don't answer. Absentmindedly I fiddle with the mugwort in my pocket, letting the crinkle and crunch soothe me.

Mom glances over. "What's that noise?"

I freeze. I'm not exactly sure how Mom would feel about the mugwort, but knowing how she reacts to most things from Halmoni . . . probably not well. "Nothing."

Her eyes narrow. "Lily, show me what's in your pocket."

Hiding it isn't worth the fight, so I pull it out and hold it flat in my palm.

She frowns. "Is that mugwort?"

"Yeah."

Mom turns back to the road as she drives, and sighs, "I'm assuming that's from Halmoni?"

The tone of her voice is a warning, but I say, "Yes."

"That's an herbal remedy that Halmoni's been taking. It helps with her nausea, but some people think it causes vivid dreams and nightmares. None of it's evidence based, of course, and it's not dangerous. But you don't need any more stress."

"Oh." I look back at the shriveled herb in my palm. I haven't dreamed anything weird. Unless the tiger was all a dream . . .

But, no. The tiger was real. I know she was.

"I'm fine," I tell her. "Halmoni said this is protection."

Mom purses her lips: the picking-her-battles face. "Okay, just be careful. Don't eat it or anything," she says. Then, "Here we are."

Mom parks and we walk past the fancy bushes and ring the fancy doorbell, and Ricky's fancy dad answers.

"Joan," he says, "nice to see you. Again."

Mom grimaces.

And I really, really don't want to say anything to Ricky's dad, but when something's wrong, you have to fix it. Especially when it's wrong because of you. "Don't blame my mom," I tell him. "She's a very good worker and doesn't do . . . strange things."

Mom looks like she can't decide if she wants to hug me or hide behind the rabbit bush.

Ricky's dad almost smiles. "I recognize that. I know what it's like to have a strange child."

I'm not sure how to respond to that, but I'll take it as a win.

"Speaking of strange kids," he says, and then calls back into the house. "Ricky, please take your friend to the den."

The phrase *Take your friend to the den* has a bit of a murder vibe to it, but when Ricky shows up, he looks sheepish. He's wearing a plain black baseball cap. It's the most normal I've ever seen him.

He gives me an uncertain wave and then leads me into the blue-themed living room. It's basically the same as the red room, only a few degrees colder. I shiver.

Ricky sits on the couch and I join him, settling into the opposite end. The cushions are lumpy and hard, and I feel like I should push my shoulders back and sit with proper posture.

"Here's your hat," I say, handing him the top hat.

He takes it without meeting my eyes and sets it between us. "Thanks."

Ricky digs a toe into the rug, looking up at the ceiling, then down at the floor—even though there's nothing interesting to see.

I clear my throat multiple times.

There's nothing more awkward than your parents forcing you to interact. It'd be fine if I'd come to apologize on my own. But this is *weird.*

On the scale of awkward-to-busy silence, this one is want-to-disappear-level bad.

I force myself to speak. "I'm sorry about the mud."

Ricky exhales. "I'm sorry, too. About the stuff we said about your grandma. I mean, your harmony."

I blink at him, confused.

"I want you to feel more comfortable, so I'm using the Korean word," he explains. "But I can stop if you want. I don't know what you want. What do you want?"

"Oh," I say. "It's *hall-moe-knee,* not *harmony.* But, yeah, you can call her whatever you want."

I didn't expect him to apologize, and now I don't know what to do.

He swallows. "I apologize for judging your culture and for being intolerant of other beliefs. I created a hostile environment, and . . ." He frowns, like he's trying to remember his lines. Then he sighs and crumples, looking at me with pain on his face. "I really am sorry. My friends and I can be kind of the worst sometimes. I know my dad thinks that. And I'm sure my teachers do. And . . . you know, everyone."

I bite my lip. Ricky's dad seems nicer than he did in the grocery store, but it's still sad that Ricky feels that way.

He takes a breath and continues. "But we really do think your hall-money is cool. Everybody in town does. And I feel really bad that she's sick. I feel really bad that I *said* she's sick. Sometimes my mouth keeps talking even when my brain knows it shouldn't."

I can't help but smile. "Thanks," I say. I didn't realize how much I was hoping to hear that. How much of a relief it is to know he doesn't think Halmoni is creepy or scary or whatever. "I don't think you're the worst. And I shouldn't have fed you mud." I mean this, mostly. But if Halmoni's right about the spell, it might not be so bad for him.

He shrugs. "Mud has vitamins, probably. I've eaten worse."

"Oh."

"A worm," he says. "Only once, though. And also another time, a Raisinet that definitely was not a Raisinet. I'm still not sure . . . Well, never mind."

I wait to see if he's joking, but he's serious. I fight back a smile. "But still. Sorry. It's not like me to do that." Then

I correct myself. "Or, I guess it is? But I didn't know that until now."

"It's okay," he says. "Let's stop apologizing now. Apologizing is awkward."

I tug at one of my braids. "Do your friends hate me?"

He laughs. "They think you're supercool. They kept referring to you as *Witch Girl.* But not in a bad way. Anyone who does something like that is probably worth knowing."

I sneak a glance at him. He's staring at me, but he looks away fast. His cheeks go splotchy.

In that moment, I don't feel like an invisible girl.

But I also don't want to be known for putting mud in someone's pudding. I wonder if there's a way to be a visible person and a good person at the same time.

"Is that going to be my reputation in school now?" I ask.

He tilts his head, thinking. "Well, yeah. But only until the next big thing."

Then after a moment, he adds, "I think it's nice that you're doing something to help your halmoni." He still says it wrong, like *hail-money,* but he's trying, and I appreciate it.

He looks at his feet before saying, "I wish I did something more, for my mom."

Oh. His *used-to* mom. Before, I thought he'd feel better

if I ignored that. But now I think talking might be good. "I'm sorry. Is she . . ."

"She's not dead. She left. Last year. And we haven't heard from her since."

I wonder if, somehow, that makes it worse. Would I feel better or worse if Dad had just left? If, instead of crashing, he'd just kept driving and never turned around? It feels wrong to think about that, but I can't help it. It's weird to think about how I could be a different person if I had Ricky's life. In a different life, how much would I change—and how much would I stay the same?

Ricky continues, "But I think, like, maybe if I did more to make her want to stay, she would have. She was a stay-at-home mom, and she always helped me with homework and stuff. Except these past couple of years, I started getting better at school, so I didn't really need help, and we didn't hang out as much, and maybe she thought I was fine without her."

"Oh. I'm really sorry." Suddenly, his self-sabotage over the language arts test and the tutoring makes sense.

He shrugs. "You don't have to say *sorry.* Everyone says *sorry,* but that doesn't help, because it's not their fault and they can't fix it."

"Well, I know that sometimes people feel trapped in their own skin, and they *have* to leave. It's part of them, and I guess you can't control that." I think of the tiger-mother and the tiger-daughter. I think of Mom and Sam. And I think of Halmoni. I almost don't trust myself to speak without my voice wobbling, but I say, "Sometimes, no matter how much you want people to stay, you have to let them go."

Ricky looks sad, but he gives me a real smile. "I've never had a friend who got it before."

"Me neither," I tell him. "It helps."

And in the spirit of *getting it*, I ask, "Do you ever feel like parts of you are changing, in a way you don't really understand?"

When he makes a face, I realize, horrifyingly, that it sounds like I'm talking about *puberty*. Quick-fast I clarify: "Not like . . . Never mind. I mean, like, you don't know who you're supposed to be anymore. And you want to figure out who you really are but you don't know how—and you're scared that you won't like the answer."

He clears his throat. "Uh, that's a deep question. I don't know. I don't feel like I have to figure that out yet. That's for when you're, like, thirty and you have a midlife crisis."

"Yeah," I say, even though I feel a flutter of embarrassment. I must sound so weird.

He shrugs. "But, I don't know, that kind of sounds like what happens in comic books. The hero is just a regular person, until suddenly the world needs them. And they have powers and a cool suit, but underneath it all, they're still trying to figure it out. They're still scared."

A strand of hair escapes my braid, and I tuck it behind my ear. "And what then? What do they do?"

He shrugs. "They save the world anyway, even though they're not ready. And they get stronger, and they learn who they are as they go along."

I nod. It's comforting that not even superheroes have it figured out. But at the same time, of course, they save the world. They're *super.*

"I think that's how you figure out who you are," Ricky says. "You do new, brave things, and you find out who *you* is in not-you situations. Does that make sense?"

"Maybe," I say.

He grins. "Yeah, well, it doesn't matter for us anyway. We don't have to worry about, you know, *the meaning of life.* The only thing we need to worry about is what's in our pudding."

I laugh. After spending so much time worrying, it's nice to be around someone who isn't afraid. Someone who believes that good things happen.

"Wait," I say. "One more question. So, if the hypothetical tiger trap didn't work, what should I do next?"

His eyebrows shoot up. "Okay, I know you vetoed the whole raw meat thing, but *hear me out—*"

"Oh boy," I say, fighting back a laugh.

He continues, "Technically, *yes,* raw meat is going to start smelling bad after a few hours. And technically, *yes,* it may attract unwanted non-tiger creatures, like rats or raccoons. Those are both fair points. But would that be worth it to accurately recreate a hypothetical tiger trap? I mean, *maybe.* Probably. Yes, yes, I think so."

Unfortunately, I already tried bait with the star jars. "I don't think bait is the answer to this problem."

His eyes narrow. "You know, this *hypothetical* stuff is getting pretty suspicious. If there's a real tiger, you know you have to tell me. Friends don't let friends *miss out on tigers.*"

"Ha. Yeah. No, it's not real. Sorry." I smile, and he sighs in disappointment.

"Well, I guess you could try making the trap somewhere else. Because, no offense, but it's pretty unlikely that a tiger would just . . . wander into your basement. Like, my great-grandfather used to go on these big hunting expeditions in the wilderness of Siberia, because that's where tigers like to be."

I nod, thinking.

"Not saying you should go to Siberia, obviously," he says. "But if you *do,* you have to take me."

I grin. "Okay, I will. I promise."

His smile fills the whole room. "We're gonna have so many adventures, Super Tiger Girl."

35

The tiger isn't there.

I'm standing in the basement, in the middle of the night, but again—it's completely empty. "Where *are* you?" I hiss.

I get nothing in response.

In my hands I hold the final star jar, and I don't know what to do. I'm so close, but I can't save Halmoni without the tiger, and the tiger is nowhere to be found.

This isn't how stories are supposed to end—right before the hero saves the day.

This isn't *fair.*

I consider what Ricky said, about going to the tiger, but where would that be? This tiger *did* just walk into my house. Where else would she go?

Frustrated, I leave the basement, and I'm just tiptoeing past the bathroom when I hear a familiar noise.

A sound like rolling thunder.

I push the bathroom door open and see Halmoni. She's sick again, but she flushes the toilet, lowers the lid, and sits on top of it.

"Come to me," she says, so I do. I set the star jar on the floor and I perch next to her on the tub.

"I hear about the mud," she says, as she dabs a wad of toilet paper at her lips.

I shake my head, ready to be done with the whole mud thing. "I already apologized to Ricky. It's fine."

She sighs. "You are little mini-me. I don't think that so good."

"But I *want* to be like you."

She balls the toilet paper up in her rice-paper hands. "Halmoni make mistakes sometime. My life not good to follow. Your life *better.*"

"But—"

"No, no," she interrupts. "Lily, my life long, long ago is growing up in a small village, so poor. We have no money. We have no food. My mom leave country when I so little, and as soon as I can, I come here to find her. But I never do. That is a sad story, Little Egg."

Gently, I take the toilet paper from her hands and toss it into the trash can. "That's why you stole from the tigers.

That's why you hid your stories away, because they were sad to think about."

She looks down at her empty hands, so delicate and fragile. She's lost so much weight. There's not much of her left.

"Lily, when I tell my story, I am sad. So much of our family story is sad. And more than that: so much of Korean people story is sad. Long, long ago, Japan and United States people do wrong things to our country. But I don't want to give you sad, angry stories. I don't want to pass you those bad feelings."

Listening to her talk, I realize there is so much of the world that I don't know. So much of my history, and so much of *me*. But I will learn it.

Because even though the tiger's stories upset me, I'm glad I heard them. They made me feel like the world is huge, and I'm filled up with it. Like I could hear the stars, and listen.

So maybe Halmoni is wrong about hiding the sad things. I've never thought she was wrong before. "But, Halmoni, maybe keeping those stories secret is the bad thing. Because all those things still happened, even if you don't talk about it. And hiding it doesn't erase the past—it only bottles it up."

She rubs my shoulder. "I think: better to forget."

"No, Halmoni, I *want* to hear your stories. If you didn't

tell me the story about the stars and how you found the tiger caves—" I pause as something dawns on me. "Wait, how did you find the tigers? How did you know where to go—where the tigers like to be?"

"I go where they keep their stories. At top of mountain."

I blow out a hot breath. Siberia. The top of a mountain. None of that helps me.

I scoot closer to her, desperation roiling inside me. "The tiger came to me, Halmoni. And she said if I freed all the stories, if I opened all the star jars, then you'd be okay again."

Her forehead crinkles. "What you saying, 'star jar'?"

"This." I spring up and lift the jar off the ground, holding it out to her. "The jars you put the stars in, when you stole them from the tigers."

She shakes her head and does that squint, like when she's lost something in her memory and can't find it. "No, little one. I think I get those here, from fly market."

"Fly market?" I blink, trying to decipher her words. And then, "You mean *flea* market? You found them at a flea market? In Sunbeam?"

She nods. "Yes, yes. Flea market. One by the coast."

"No," I say, holding the star jar closer to her face, like I can force her to remember. "They're from Korea. You hid magical star stories in them. And you hid them in the boxes. That's why you were so nervous about moving the boxes . . . because the jars are magic."

"Everything a little bit magic," Halmoni says, slowly. "But those just jars."

I shake my head. Maybe she's having one of her forgetting episodes, because this doesn't make sense. "These star jars are magic. They *have* to be."

"Lily Bean," she murmurs. Her eyes are clear. This isn't like her other episodes, where she looked all foggy, but I don't understand. I don't get how this is possible.

"I opened the first two jars, and the tiger told me the stories," I say. "There's just one left, and once I get to the end, you'll be healed. I can save you."

"Aii-yah." She takes my hand in hers, rubbing my life line, like she always does. "Lily Bean, I don't need saving. I not scare anymore."

"But this will work. The tiger said—"

"Tigers speak in tricky ways. Not always meaning what we want."

I shake my head, because I don't want her to speak in confusing, tiger-like riddles. I want her to *listen.* "You don't get it. This is your last chance. I have to do this. You have to get better."

Her eyes are so dark, so shadowed. "No, you stop. You listen. *This* is end, Lily. This my time."

"You can't just give up, though!" I yank my hand

away from her. She can't pretend to comfort me, when she's really saying horrible things.

She looks down. "When I younger and missing my mom, I use to think she is a monster for leaving me. I use to be so mad. But now I understand. Sometime you have to leave you little ones, even though you don't want to. Sometime you know it is time."

"But it's not time!" My voice cracks, but I shout anyway. "You have to keep fighting! You're supposed to be strong."

Halmoni winces, like our conversation physically pains her. "There is too much fighting already. No more of that."

I squeeze my eyes so tightly that I see stars, exploding behind my eyelids. "But I've been working so hard. I'm so close. There has to be a point to all of this. There has to be a happy ending. . . ."

"Go to bed, little one," she says softly. "No more."

36

I walk up to the attic room, holding the little blue jar in my hands. The jar feels heavy. I feel heavy.

I was brave. I was strong.

And now it's all for nothing? The tiger is gone, and Halmoni is done.

How can I fight so hard if she has already given up?

"Where are you?" I whisper when I reach the top of the stairs.

Sam snuck out again tonight. The room feels quiet without her snores. The house feels big without the tiger.

When I get no response, I pull the two empty star jars out from under my bed, gathering the three of them in my arms. My heart thumps in my chest. And the walls around me seem to thump as well—an angry pounding sound, like the whole house is mad at Halmoni.

"I brought these to you," I call out to a tiger who isn't there. "You said you would help."

Silence, still, except for the pounding, and I'm so *angry.*

Louder, I shout, "How could you disappear? How could you just leave me alone?"

The thumping around me gets louder, coming from the window now, and I turn, expecting the tiger—but it's Sam. Her head pops up outside the window, and she hoists herself inside, red faced and panting.

I realize that the thumping was her, climbing up the rope.

She slings her backpack off her shoulders, dumping it onto the floor. It's not zipped properly, and a plastic bag slides out. It seems like it's filled with rice, but in the moonlight, I can't exactly tell.

Sam catches her breath. "I told you. I just had to get out. I'm not *leaving* you."

"I wasn't talking to you," I say.

She squints and then tilts her head, staring at the jars in my arms. "Where'd you get those vases?"

"They aren't *vases.* They're . . ."

She raises an eyebrow and gives me a look like I am the strangest little kid ever.

"Never mind." Honestly: How dare she come in now?

How dare she shrug and look at these jars like *whatever*? How dare she act so careless when I care so much?

I don't exactly *plan* to do this. I don't really think it through. But.

I take the green jar and throw it, and it explodes against the wall.

She shrieks. "What are you *doing*?"

And you know what? It feels good to break it.

It's just too *much*—all that hope and fear and strength and power. All those stories, and consequences, and uncertainty. It's all too much to keep bottled up inside me.

I lift the tall, thin jar—and I throw it against the wall, watching with relief as that one shatters, too.

"Stop," Sam shouts. "STOP."

"I was trying to help her," someone shouts, way too loud, and I realize it's me, but it doesn't sound like me.

It's like I am possessed. Or cursed. Or something.

I am thunder and lightning. I am out of control.

The only jar left is the little blue one—the last one. The jar that's still filled with the final story.

It's my last chance. It's Halmoni's last chance.

I have to get it to the tiger before it's too late. Except maybe—the thing is—what if—it's already too late?

And what if none of this ever meant anything in the first place? What if impossible things—talking tigers, trapping stars, saving your halmoni—really are impossible?

Maybe all of this was just a mugwort dream or a mental stress reaction after all. Maybe jars are just jars. Maybe I wanted it to be okay so badly that I made everything up.

I throw the last star jar.

It shatters.

37

Back in fifth grade, during our astronomy unit, we learned about stars and galaxies and black holes. But my favorite thing was the supernova—a star exploding, bigger than we could ever imagine. An infinite, powerful force, like the sun swallowing itself whole.

Here, now, I create my own. Shattering against the wall, the blue jar becomes a supernova. I can't contain myself. All that fear, all that anger, all that lost hope—

Someone grabs my arm, and I look up to see Mom. Her eyes are scared, but then she wraps me up, holds me to her and keeps me from falling to pieces.

Sam presses herself against the wall, face pale. I wonder what she sees, looking at me. Not a QAG anymore, but what? A wild girl, maybe. Half tiger.

The thunder and lightning are gone, and only the rain

is left. I gasp for air. "I wanted to help. I wanted to believe."

Mom squeezes me tight, and I try to shove her away. She holds me tighter, and I push harder—and then I stop pushing. I let her hold me.

"It's okay," she says.

Footsteps thud up the stairs, and Halmoni appears in the doorway. She looks pale, as withered as dried mugwort, and she shakes, unsteady on her feet.

"Girls," she breathes.

And she collapses.

38

"*Sam,*" Mom barks. "Phone."

Sam fumbles in her pocket, hands shaking as she passes the phone to Mom. Then she kneels beside Halmoni.

I stand, staring at the Halmoni-heap, watching Sam check her pulse.

It's hard to breathe. I know now: The moment when everything really falls apart—it's not during the big explosion. It's in the quiet right after. And the feeling is not a shattering. Not quite.

It's more of a crumbling. Like I'm still trying to hold my heart together, but the tighter I squeeze, the faster it breaks apart.

Crumble, crumble, until there's nothing but tiny pieces, scraps of feeling that I can't put back together.

I cross my arms around myself as Mom calls 911. She

recites Halmoni's address and says, *Yes, yes, yes, please. Please.* Her voice is breathless, and as soon as she hangs up, she drops to the floor, tossing the phone to the side and throwing her arms over Halmoni, murmuring something I can't hear.

I inch closer, trying to catch her words—but I am afraid to get too close. Sam looks up at me, and Mom's words blur together, *I'm sorry I'm sorryI'msorry.*

This is my fault. I shouldn't have stressed Halmoni out. Halmoni's allowed to have moments of weakness, of wanting to give up, but I should have been strong.

When the paramedics arrive, they sweep Halmoni onto a stretcher and out of the attic, out of the house, down the forever steps. Sam and I follow Mom into the living room, but she stops us.

"Wait here," she says to Sam. "Watch your sister."

Then she runs outside, after Halmoni—and they are gone, carried away by flashing lights and sirens.

Sam and I are left with silence.

We stand with our arms wrapped around ourselves, staring out the window at the empty street.

"Our family is broken," Sam says.

I broke it, I do not say.

"Is she going to be okay?" I ask instead.

The rain beats against the windows.

When Sam finally does speak, there's a hint of tears in her eyes, shining like stars. "What if this is my fault?"

"What do you mean?" She's not the one who broke the jars.

"I said I hoped she would die soon. I didn't knock on wood." Her chest shudders. "But I didn't mean it. I tried to undo it. I've been scattering rice at night because Halmoni said it could protect us, but it didn't work."

My heart squeezes. The rice—in Sam's backpack, spilled on the floor—it makes sense now. That's where she was going at night. Sam still believed, even when she tried not to.

I didn't realize she was hoping, too.

"It wasn't you," I whisper. "It wasn't your fault."

She rubs her hands over her face. "We should go, right? Follow them to the hospital?"

But following them seems like admitting: this is the end. "Mom told us to stay here," I say.

Sam ignores me. "I'll call Jensen. She'll drive us."

"Jensen?" I ask, completely confused. Jensen's nice and all, but she barely knows us, and it's the middle of the night.

Sam calls, but she gets voice mail and hangs up. "She's probably still driving. She never checks her phone when she drives."

"Why would Jensen be driving? She's probably *sleeping*."

"She was helping me scatter the rice," Sam says. "She's been helping me."

"Oh." All this was happening and I had no idea.

Sam stares out the window, at the rain. "Lily, I think I have to drive us?"

"You don't have to if you're scared," I say. "But if you're ready . . . yeah, I think we should go to her."

I know Sam's as scared as I am. But I know she'll be brave anyway, because she's my sister.

Sam swallows. "Are you ready?"

I nod.

Sam grabs Mom's car keys from the kitchen counter. I throw the front door open, and the storm welcomes us with a howl.

Then we run down the stairs. Down and down, together.

39

The rain is relentless. We can hardly see the road.

Sam drives slowly, leaning forward, gripping the steering wheel, squinting at the road ahead.

We inch forward—until Sam starts shaking. She pulls the car over to the side of the road and parks.

We don't make it far. We're just out of Halmoni's driveway, right in front of the library.

"What happened?" I ask.

She's still shaking. "I know Mom gets mad at me about not driving, but every time I get in the car, I think about Dad."

We have to get to the hospital, and fast. But Sam won't drive, and I won't force her to.

Softly, so I can barely hear it, Sam says, "I can't go

through this again. People always say someone lives on in your memory, but we can't remember everything, and if we can't keep the memory alive, then that's it. The person you loved is gone."

What is left of someone when the memories fade? Do you carry a halmoni, or a dad, in your heart, even after you forget the stories—even if you never knew them? "I don't remember Dad," I tell her.

"But that's not your fault. I'm the one who failed, because I was old enough to remember him." She takes a shaky breath. "When Dad died, I made a list that I recited every night. The little things about him, you know?

"Like, he cracked his knuckles constantly. His eyes watered whenever he ate kimchi, but he still insisted on eating it. He read us his favorite picture books every night before bed, even when I got too old for them."

I stare at her. She's never told me this before. And I feel a flicker of recognition in my heart—like a tiger lifting its head inside me. I remember Dad reading to us—*If You Give a Mouse a Cookie, Where the Wild Things Are, Goodnight Moon.*

I feel the echo of his voice, lines from storybooks, hidden in my brain. Dad's there, almost.

"I was so afraid of forgetting something," Sam says, voice cracking. "But of course I have. I know I have."

"Why didn't you tell me? Why didn't you share the

list?" Maybe I could have known him, through Sam. I could have helped her remember him.

Then Sam, my fearless sister, my sister with the sharp teeth and sharper words—starts to cry. Soft first, a drizzle, then a storm. "I didn't want to share. Like, if I told you all those Dad-stories, they'd disappear. They wouldn't be mine anymore."

"Stories don't belong to anybody," I say. "They're meant to be told."

Maybe it's scary to tell stories and share their truths—but I'd rather face them than run.

I take a breath. It's my turn to say a scary thing. "I saw this tiger, and she spoke to me, and she told me she could heal Halmoni. I really believed that the magic was real, but now I'm afraid that it wasn't. Maybe I was hoping too hard, and it was all just a mental stress reaction, like you said. I thought I could be a hero, that I didn't have to be a QAG anymore."

Sam wipes the black smudges from her face. "The QAG thing . . . that was stupid. I shouldn't have put that stereotype on you. And I shouldn't have said the tiger wasn't real. Maybe I was wrong. Maybe, somehow, it *is* real. I want to believe that. And maybe we *have* to believe."

Her eyes shimmer with tears. "That's what I've always admired about you. You don't give up on magic. And I was wrong to tell you to."

I stare out the windshield. What would it mean to hope, now, at the very end? When Sam can't drive in the rain, and we're stuck, and Halmoni is dying and we can't get to her?

"Lily," Sam says. "Remember when you asked me about the tiger story? About whether I would run?"

I close my eyes and nod.

"I want you to know, whenever we can't run, whenever you have to stand and face it—I'll be here. I'll stand with you."

I get that filled-up feeling. We are the sun and the moon, ready to be brave. And sometimes, believing is the bravest thing of all.

But none of that matters. Sam can't drive in the rain, so we're stuck. Halmoni is dying and we can't get to her.

Yes, we're trapped, but then something surfaces in my memory.

I have an idea.

40

Ricky said to go to a place that tigers like. Halmoni said she went where tigers kept their stories.

And when I was making the mud pudding, the tiger said that the library was her favorite place.

The *library*, a home for stories.

"Wait here," I tell Sam. Then I fly out of the car and run toward the library.

The door is locked. Because it's the middle of the night, so of course. But I won't let that stop me. Not now.

I try one of the windows, but it doesn't open. And I feel hopeless until I remember: Mom, outside Halmoni's house.

It's a long shot, I know, but I tap the side of the pane, run my hands over the windowsill, and thump a fist right below the glass.

I hold my breath and think, *Please*. Then I push.

Like a miracle, the window opens.

Sam shouts my name, and I spin around to see her standing behind me. "I told you to wait in the car."

She bug-eyes me. "Are you kidding? You're breaking into the library and I'm supposed to wait in the car?"

"Please, I just—I need to do this on my own. It won't take very long."

She shakes her head slowly. "If I just sit by while you break into a building, I'm basically the worst older sister of all time—"

I lean forward and squeeze her in a hug, and she's so surprised she stops talking. "You're the best sister. But I need you to wait in the car and be ready to go. Just trust me."

She runs her hand through her hair. "Oh my god. Okay. Okay, fine. I will be your getaway driver, even though you realize I *can't drive in the rain*."

"Thank you," I say, and then I pull myself up and through the window, tumbling into the library.

"Please be in here," I whisper once I'm inside.

It's dark, but I am Little Eggi. I am the sun, and the dark doesn't scare me anymore.

I weave through the stacks. "Hello?"

My chest clenches because I thought the tiger would be here. I was so *sure*. Yet, the library is silent.

"Hello!" I call again. The quiet is so loud I can't stand it. I sweep all the books off the nearest shelf, and they crash to the ground. "Please just come out! I need your help!"

"All right, fine." It's her voice, and I spin around to see my tiger lying in a corner, head resting on her paws.

"You're here," I breathe. I feel ridiculous, like I could almost cry. She's a terrifying beast, but it feels so good to see her. There's still hope.

"You owe me an apology," she says. "I am not a monster. You cannot wish me away like a bad dream."

"I'm sorry," I say. "I don't know if you're good or bad, and I don't know if I'm doing the right thing."

I'm going off a hunch—an idea that's just barely formed—a spark, a hope. But I decide to be brave. "I noticed something, when I saw you that night after the grocery store. I didn't really think about it before, but . . . it seemed like the rain wasn't falling around you. And I thought you were there to hurt Halmoni, but now I think . . . maybe you were standing there to guide us home."

When she doesn't respond, I swallow hard and add, "And I really hope I'm right. I really hope you have that magic. Because I need your help."

She stands slowly, and I think I hear her bones creak, but it could be the trees outside, whipping in the storm.

"Follow me," she says. And she leads me through the stacks, out of the library.

I run back to the car, slam the door, and fasten my seat belt. "I think she wants us to follow," I say.

Outside, the tiger steps in front of our car and turns, slowly, until she's facing away from us. Her tail flick-flicks low to the ground, almost kissing the pavement.

Then she steps forward, moving in slow motion like she has all the time in the world, one claw, one paw, one leg at a time. As she walks, the rain lessens behind her. It doesn't stop completely, but now the rain is just a drizzle.

Everywhere around us, the rain is still heavy, except for the path the tiger clears.

I don't understand weather patterns. Maybe this can be explained away by clouds and wind and whatever. But this feels like something different. This feels like magic.

"She, who? What's happening?" Sam breathes, eyes wide. She may not see the tiger, but she sees the drizzly path, cleared just for us. "Is it the tiger?"

I hesitate, then nod.

"I don't see her," she whispers. There's disbelief and fear in her voice—but underneath it all, a hint of longing. She tugs at her white streak and pushes it behind her ear. "Why don't I see her?"

I never understood it before—why Sam was so angry about all Halmoni's traditions. About the magic. But now I think it's because she wanted, so badly, to be a part of it. And maybe she was afraid she couldn't be, so she pushed it all away.

I reach up to unclasp my pendant, then lean over to fasten it around her neck. Extra protection. Extra love. Just in case.

"We'll be okay," I tell her. "Sometimes, believing is the bravest thing of all. Now drive."

41

My tiger leads us to the hospital.

"That was . . . You are . . . ," Sam says as she parks, but she shakes her head. There's no time.

We run out of the car, past the tiger, and in through the automatic sliding doors.

Hospitals are cold and bright. The smell of rubbing alcohol stings my nose, like it's trying to disinfect my nostrils. In here, everything is clean, controlled. The outside is wild with rain and wind and tigers, but inside, nature can't touch us.

Sam talks to somebody at the front desk of the emergency room, and a nurse takes us through the hospital, twisting and turning through white hallways.

Then she drops us off at Halmoni's room.

Mom lies with Halmoni on the bed, curled up next to

her. She's blocking our view of Halmoni, but I hear her whisper, "I'll give you whatever you want. Just don't take her. Not yet."

I don't know if she's praying to a god or a tiger or something in between.

Sam knocks on the open door, and when Mom looks up, I expect anger. She told us to stay home, and Sam drove here with only a learner's permit. We broke the law, and worse—we broke Mom's rule.

But Mom's too tired for scolding. "I was going to call you girls soon. It doesn't look good."

I want to ask her what that means, but I also don't want to know. And also, I think I *do* know.

She motions Sam and me into the room, but I stay in the doorway.

Halmoni looks small in the hospital bed, pale against the light blue blanket. She wears a thin oxygen tube, but with her sequined head scarf, she's glamorous, even now. Even when she looks sick.

No.

Sick is not the right word.

Sick is Halmoni throwing up in the bathroom. *Sick* is Sam's pink nose when she has the flu. *Sick* is my sore, swollen throat when I got strep.

This is not *sick*. This is *not getting better.*

Halmoni looks like she's dying.

And I'm not ready.

I take a step backward, but Halmoni opens her eyes and sees us. "Sam," she says. Her voice is small. "I talk to Sam first."

Sam's voice is a squeak. "Me? Really?"

Halmoni nods weakly, and Sam rushes to her side.

Mom walks over to me. "Come on. Let's get some snacks from the vending machine."

I follow her out, but the bright lights and the smell of the hospital make me dizzy. I don't want to be in the place where Halmoni will die.

Mom walks ahead, assuming that I'm following, but I turn myself invisible and walk the opposite way, away from Mom and Halmoni, down the winding halls, until I'm back outside the sliding doors, until I can breathe.

I stand under the canopy outside the hospital entrance. In front of me, the tiger is sitting in the rain, like I knew she would be.

An invisible girl and an invisible tiger. We match.

"I think I know how the stories changed me," I tell her.

Her ears twitch. "How?"

I inhale. "They made me want all these opposite things at the same time. I don't know how I can feel so many things at once. And I don't know which feelings and which wants are right."

"What do you want, Lily?"

My heart beats. I get that filled-up, bursting feeling again. And then I say, "I want Halmoni to live longer, but I also don't want her to hurt longer.

"And I want—" My voice cracks, and I don't think I can keep going, but I do. "I want to go back into that room, to be with Halmoni and my family, but I also want to run very far away."

I take a breath. The rain falls.

I tell her, "I hate all this wanting. I get why the tiger-girl begged for a cure. It's terrible to feel so *much.*"

She shifts her weight, and her stripes glow. "The tiger-girl was wrong, Lily. As it turns out, she quite likes her tiger form. And she knows, now, that you can be more than one thing. If you are strong, you can hold more than one truth in your heart."

I shake my head. "Well, I'm not strong. I'm not ready for the end of Halmoni's story. I can't face it."

"Lily, I told you I would heal my Ae-Cha, but healing is not always about curing illness. Often, it is about understanding. And when you face your whole story, you can understand your whole heart."

My whole heart hurts. "I messed it up. I didn't know if it was real or not, and I was angry, and I broke the jar. The final story is gone, and now Halmoni won't even have that."

"It's not gone," she says. "You released it. And I cannot

tell it to you, but you know more than you realize. These are the stories of our family, after all."

I pause, turning her words over. *My Ae-Cha. Our family.* My family, and hers. "Are you . . . Halmoni's mom? Am I . . . ?" I don't say *a tiger-girl,* because I don't have to. I already know.

She doesn't answer my questions. "Take your history, understand where you came from and who you are—then find your own story. Create the story of who you are yet to be."

Before I can respond, the doors slide open. I turn to see an Asian nurse with pink scrubs and orange lipstick. "There you are!" she says. "Your mother is in a panic over you. Come on now."

I look back to my tiger, but she's gone, like I knew she would be.

42

The nurse leads me down the white hallways again, and I have to hurry to keep up with her. "I'm really sorry," she says once we reach the door. "I still remember when I said goodbye to my grandmother. It's so hard. But I'm praying for you, honey."

Mom sees us and runs over. "Lily. You scared me! You can't run off like that! Especially not now." She pulls my head toward her and breathes me in. "Okay. Halmoni wants to talk to you."

My mind swirls with the tiger's words.

I take a breath and I step inside, toward Halmoni.

Sam stands. She doesn't bother wiping away tears, but she rubs my arm as she passes and leaves the room. Then it's just me and Halmoni and the hospital machines, beeping next to us.

I half-moon my palms with my fingernails, and I sit on the gray hospital chair beside the bed. It's scratchy, and the fabric *skritch-skritch*es against my thighs.

"Lily Bean." Halmoni's hand twitches in a way that seems almost inhuman. That seems wrong. And I'm scared and sad, and a piece of me wants to turn away. But I grab her hand, and those feelings don't disappear, and I realize there's love there, too, and that's stronger than anything else.

"I am seeing the truth," Halmoni says. "I see my mother. My umma. She finally find me."

"Halmoni," I whisper, "I think I saw her, too."

Halmoni smiles. "You always see, Little Egg. That is you power."

My chest hurts, but I squeeze her hand, tracing her life line with my thumb.

"All my life, I spend *so* much time, *so* much energy, hiding my heart. I am scare of tigers. But more, I am scare of the tiger in me," she says. "I thought I have to hide my words, because my English not so good. I thought I have to hide my heart, because I feel too much. And I thought I have to hide my story, because I think if I tell it, it is who I am forever." She takes a shallow breath. "But when I keep it tight-tight, it eat me up. I don't see the love, all around me."

Hope rages inside me, even though I try to stop it. Even though I know how dangerous it is. "Maybe everything can be okay, now that you realize that. You can heal now."

"I am ready now."

My throat feels swollen shut. "I'm not."

She closes her eyes. "Sometime, the strongest thing is to stop running. To say, *I am not afraid of tigers. I am not afraid to die.*"

But I'm so afraid.

For a fraction of a second, I see a flash of a tiger's face beneath her expression—

It's gone almost as soon as I see it, but I know what I saw. It's the fierceness in her, the courage she'll have in her next chapter.

She will be brave.

Sam and Mom come back then, and Sam sits on the other side of the bed and holds Halmoni's other hand. Mom walks over and rubs my back.

With her eyes still closed and her lips lifted into the smallest smile, Halmoni says, whisper-fierce, "Tell me a story."

Sam looks at me and reaches up with one hand. She makes a grasping motion, as if she's plucking a star from the sky, and holds it out to me.

At the edges of my mind, a story starts to form—it comes together from mist and shadow. It takes shape.

I scoot toward Halmoni—

closer—

closer—

and I begin.

43

Long, long ago, when tiger drank the stars, ten thousand suns and ten thousand moons after a girl stole stories from tigers—two little girls lived with their halmoni in a house on a hill. They were sisters, one with long black braids, one with dark eye makeup. Once, they'd shared everything, but over time, they'd grown apart—grown alone.

One day, the halmoni went to the village to buy rice and Happy Nut crackers for her girls, but she got trapped in traffic. She got home late, much later than usual.

The sky was dark that night—rain clouds covered the stars—and when the halmoni passed by the windows, her shadow shifted, taking the shape of a tiger.

It may have been a trick of the dark, but they could not tell.

Little girls, *the halmoni said,* let me in.

The sisters peeked through the window, but that night, their halmoni looked different. She was transformed.

The sisters were afraid. They didn't know what to do. So they tried to change her back. Unya scattered the rice, and Eggi spilled the stars. They tried everything, but nothing worked.

Finally, when there was nothing left but the end of the story. A sky god saw them and took pity.

See, centuries before, a different sky god had created a tiger-girl who walked both worlds.

Even the gods make mistakes, but as it turned out, the mistake hadn't been the tiger-girl at all.

The mistake was making her choose. The mistake was creating a world where she had to hide—where she was afraid to be everything at once, fierce and kind, soft and strong.

But that was an old god, with old ways, and the new god recognized her family—her great-granddaughters.

So she dropped a staircase for Little Egg. And a rope for Unya.

Come, *said the new sky god.* There is something I want you to see.

In the hospital room, I taste salt, and I realize I'm crying. I look up and see Sam. I feel Mom's touch on my back.

Beneath my fingertips, Halmoni's pulse gets weaker, fading away.

"Keep going," Sam whispers.

The seconds swell. I take a breath. There are so many endings to choose from. And I find mine.

Together, the two sisters climbed up and up, and when they reached the sky god, a sky tiger, she showed them a galaxy filled with jars. Some jars had been carried across the world, long hidden. Others had traveled across the sea, to a flea market by the coast, hoping to find their family. And all of these jars released the truth and longing and love.

Open them, *the tiger said.*

The girls were scared, but they were brave, too. They believed in hope. They opened the jars and stories. Some were scary, some were sad, but the girls only felt proud, because this was the story of their family—generations of women who'd fought for their hearts. Women who could be everything and anything.

Now you can tell your own star stories, *the sky tiger told them, her voice* skritch*ing like coarse fabric against their ears.* Light is not limited.

So the sisters began to speak. They told stories of their halmoni, who always wore sequins, and always saw her granddaughters. Who risked everything for happiness, and did anything to protect her family. Who believed in invisible things—like spirits and magic and love.

The girls talked about their halmoni, who'd taught them to see the world, and to see themselves.

As they spoke, they filled the sky with stars. The sisters lit the world.

And in the light, they found their way back home.

In the light, they saw: They were not alone.

44

When I finish my story, Halmoni is smiling. Her eyes are closed and her pulse flutters, barely anything anymore.

"I love you," I tell her.

I squeeze one of Halmoni's hands. Sam squeezes the other. Mom strokes her hair.

This is the end. But it doesn't happen right away, not like in the movies.

Over the next few hours, her breath becomes softer and softer. We watch as she fades.

"The stories were supposed to save her," I say in a small voice.

Mom makes a noise, and when I look at her, there are tears in her eyes. "They did save her, Lily. They reminded her that the world is big. That she could be anything. That she was everything to us."

Halmoni looks so pale, lying on the bed. So helpless.

"I'm scared," I say.

"I know," Mom says, "but you're not alone."

Sam reaches up to unclasp the pendant. She takes it in her palm, presses it into mine, and intertwines our fingers.

Together we hold our little piece of magic—our piece of Halmoni.

"It's okay," I whisper, leaning so close to Halmoni that my lips brush her ear. I close my eyes and breathe. Sometimes, the bravest thing is to stop running. "It's okay if you go. We will be all right."

I don't know, for sure, if she hears me. But I think she does. The room seems to sigh in relief.

I look up, and the world outside is dark, but through the window, two small spots of light blink back at me. It's hard to see. It's hard to know for sure. It could be the reflection of the machines inside, or it could be tiger eyes, staring back at me.

I watch them, my heart clenching tight like a little fist. And then they disappear, blinking closed. Something opens up inside me, a hole that wasn't there before. An emptiness and a loss, but also . . . *space.* An open jar, a release.

I lean my head against Halmoni's heart, and I sit in that small room with my family.

When Halmoni finally does go, I know she's ready. She has always been brave.

45

The basement is flooded.

The first night, after we return to Halmoni's house, Mom throws the basement door open and shakes her head. Water laps at the steps. The boxes that Ricky and I worked so hard to stack slowly disintegrate into mush. Mom stares at the water for a long, long time before calling someone to get it fixed.

The second night, Mom decides to sleep in Halmoni's room. Sam lies awake, biting her fingernails. And the rest of the house goes quiet. The floorboards don't whine beneath my feet. The doors don't sing. Without Halmoni, the house is just a house. A too-quiet, too-empty house that none of us know how to live in.

The days pass quietly. The hours go blurry.

Ricky texts me a continuous stream of his favorite

foods, trying to cheer me up. And on the seventh night, after one official week, he texts: *rice cakes.*

When I read the words, the threat of tears burns behind my eyes. I almost turn my phone off and hide beneath my covers.

But his text reminds me of something. An important date rattles around in my head. On my phone, I check the calendar, and I see: tomorrow is the bake sale.

I have an idea, and for the first time all week, the heaviness in my chest lifts a little. I tell Ricky my plan, then text Jensen before throwing my blankets back.

I run down the attic steps, not bothering with invisibility. Banging around the kitchen, gathering pots and pans, I fill our home with noise. The house begins to wake.

Mom comes into the kitchen, with Sam trailing her.

"What are you doing?" Sam blinks.

"Rice cakes. For the bake sale."

Sam's confused, but Mom doesn't question it. She walks over to me and starts pulling ingredients off the shelf—a jar of mochi flour, a box of sugar, adzuki bean paste.

Sam says, "We don't have to do the bake sale."

"We don't have to," I say, looking between her and Mom. "But . . . maybe we should. All that food. All those people. It'll be like . . ."

Understanding settles on Sam's face, and her eyes ache with grief. "Like a kosa."

"At the library," Mom says. For a moment, she looks too pained to speak, but she does. "The library was one of Halmoni's projects, so many years ago. She painted it bright colors and added cheesy posters. She always wanted it to be a special place."

I stare at her, wondering how, all this time, I never knew.

But I don't have much time to process that, because Sam asks Mom, "Do you know how to make the rice cakes?"

Mom nods, but a bit of panic slips into her voice. "Uh, I think. Maybe. Vaguely." And then, softer, "I never thought to ask."

I think of the time when I asked Halmoni for her recipe—she said *later.* And now it's too late.

But Mom looks hopeful, and I take a breath.

"It's okay," I say. "Even if things aren't perfect, they can still be good."

Mom squeezes my shoulder, and we begin, measuring flour and coconut milk based on what feels right. And cooking together, mashing our hands into mochi batter—that feels right.

46

Ricky and Jensen have spread the word. Nearly the whole town comes to the library for Halmoni's kosa. Halmoni's friends fill the room with food and stories. People come up to us, tell us how sorry they are, how much they loved her—people we don't even know, people Halmoni helped or healed.

Joe finds me, and at first I apologize. He isn't charging for the bake-sale-turned-kosa, of course. So the whole plan to save the library is ruined. "I know we were supposed to raise money," I say.

Joe shakes his head. "This wasn't for money. This was for community. Though maybe later we can discuss the break-in."

My cheeks get hot. "How'd you know about that?"

"Intuition," he replies. "And the kid-sized muddy footprints everywhere."

"Oh." I kind of forgot about that.

But his mustache twitches, and he smiles softly. "Heartbreak is often messy." He hands me a cookie, and I thank him.

Across the library, Mom talks to a few adults I don't recognize, and Sam finds her way to Jensen. Jensen takes Sam in her arms and kisses the top of her head, and Sam leans against Jensen's neck. There's a love between them that confuses me for a moment.

And suddenly it all makes sense. Sam's weirdness when she first saw Jensen. The nervousness when Sam asked me about her later. The way Jensen helped Sam scatter rice, the way Sam tried to call her for help.

They're a couple.

I'm stunned, even though now it seems obvious. They're a good match. Jensen is nice, and Sam is soft with her, and they fit.

On the other side of the library, I see Ricky with his friends. They all wave to me, and Ricky abandons them for a moment, walking up to me with a wicker basket in his arms. He's wearing a black bowler hat today, a glamorous one that Halmoni would have loved.

"Chocolate muffins," he explains. "Joe gave me his recipe." And then, with a tilted smile: "I promise, no mud."

He holds out the basket, the great-grandson of a tiger hunter offering baked goods to the great-granddaughter of a tiger god.

I accept it, and warmth spreads up my fingertips and through my body. A small part of me perks up, smiles. And I'm not sure the smile reaches my face, but maybe this is how healing starts—small bits of happiness waking up inside you, until maybe one day it spreads through your whole self.

"I passed my language arts test," he says. "So we'll be in the same grade in the fall."

I smile, for real this time. "That's great, Ricky."

He grins, and when I excuse myself, he gets it. He knows I'm not ready for a full conversation yet.

I slip out the heavy front doors and sit on the steps, cradling the muffins on my lap.

I think about our conversation before, about learning who you are, even in not-you situations. I've been doing that, pushing back the edges of me—trying to find the borders—and I'm realizing that I'm so much more than I thought. Right now, I feel infinite.

I take a bite of a muffin—and then cough, spitting it into my palm. *Salt*. Ricky must have mixed the sugar up with the salt.

The unexpected flavor shocks a laugh out of me.

"Can I sit?" someone asks.

At first, I think the voice is the tiger's. I keep expecting to hear her, or catch a glimpse of her out of the corner of my eye. But I also know, deep down—she's gone.

When I turn, I see Sam, who sits down next to me without waiting for a response. She reaches into the basket, grabbing a muffin without asking.

"I wouldn't—" I say, but it's too late. Sam's already choking on her bite, spitting her own mouthful into her palm. She stares at me, and I laugh, and she laughs—

And then we stop, abruptly, dumping the chewed-up muffins back into the basket.

It feels wrong, to be happy right now.

"Does it get easier?" I ask. "Does the sadness go away?"

Sam stares ahead. "The sadness fades, yeah. Eventually. But the missing . . . I don't know if that ever does."

I press my thumb against my palm, and when I close my eyes, I can almost imagine it's Halmoni, tracing my life line, telling me everything is going to be okay. The evening air heats my skin. It finally feels like August, and I fill my lungs with warmth.

Sam scoots closer, until our arms touch. In the sky, the sun is setting, and the moon peeks over the trees. "Will you tell me another story?" she asks.

I breathe in. The seconds swell. I find my voice.

"Long, long ago . . . ," I begin.

I don't yet know the ending, but I will face my story as it changes and grows. Because of Halmoni, I can be brave. I can be anything.

I am a girl who sees invisible things, but I am not invisible.

Author's Note

When I was little, my halmoni told me stories.

My younger sister and I would curl up in bed with her, and as she spoke of ghosts and tigers, our world filled with magic. In those moments, I would have sworn I heard tigers outside the bedroom, their sharp claws *skritch*ing against the wood floors. I could practically see their shadows seeping under the door.

On those nights, I felt connected to a line of Korean women I'd never known—as if their stories still lived in my blood. When I listened to Halmoni, I wasn't part white, part Asian, one-quarter Korean, mixed. I was just full me, and I knew it in my bones.

Years later, when I left Hawaii for college, I abandoned the stories—not intentionally, just by accident, as though they'd slid under my bed and gathered dust. Before long, I forgot they were missing.

I didn't know how much I needed them until late in college, when somebody asked if I was Korean.

Just a quarter, I answered. The words felt wrong as soon as I spoke them. The answer, quite simply, has always been *yes.* But somewhere along the way, I'd started dividing my blood into parts.

Wanting to be whole again, I turned back to the stories, reading old fairy tales and searching the internet—but they were different now. These were not my halmoni's stories. Somehow they had shape-shifted. Maybe they had changed. Maybe I couldn't find them. Maybe my halmoni had told different versions, and invented some entirely.

When I asked her to recall her stories, she waved her hand. *Oh, so long ago,* she said. *I don't know what I say.*

So, with nowhere else to turn, I wrote my own story.

I started with my favorite: two siblings run from a tiger, escaping into the sky to become the sun and the moon. It's a popular story, with many variations, but I always felt like the story was hiding something—and I wanted to know its secrets.

The tiger in that story is clever and determined. It dresses up as the children's grandmother. It hunts them down. It attempts to trick them, and when that doesn't work, it chases them far and wide. It tries to chase them into the sky.

The tiger is ceaseless in its pursuit, and I always wondered, what does it want? Nothing so crass as meat; this felt like more. What could be so important, so powerful, that the tiger would chase these children across the world?

I wrote a dozen drafts in search of the answer, but it did not come easily. It was as if I had to prove I was trustworthy before the story would reveal its secrets.

So I worked for it. I dug back through my family history and the history of Korea.

I read about colonialism and oppression, about a hidden language and forgotten stories, about comfort women and imposed silence. But in this dark history, I found strength, too. Korean people—Korean women, in particular—are fierce and resilient, and as I worked, I understood my halmoni and myself better.

My research revealed strange coincidences. In an early draft, I'd written about star jars full of magic, without really knowing why. The idea had seemed to come out of nowhere.

Later, I discovered Chilseong, or the Seven Stars—a deity that watches over children and is often honored by the setting out of bowls or jars.

Similarly, in my story I'd invented a small Korean island where the sea parts once a year. While poring over a map of Korea, trying to find a place for my fictional village, I learned that it already exists—Jindo, a seaside island where once a year, due to a combination of tides and maybe just a bit of magic, the ocean really does part.

I worked like this, alternating between writing and research, treating these coincidences as clues, as if I were piecing together a story that had already been told long, long ago and I only had to bridge the gaps.

I worked my way through history, all the way back to the Korean origin myth. And there I found the biggest coincidence.

Before my research, I'd had a vague understanding of the origin myth, but for some reason, my halmoni had never told us this one. It goes like this:

Long, long ago, there was a heavenly prince who ruled over Earth. His job was easy enough until a bear and a tiger, tired of their wild lives, asked him to turn them human.

He said that if they lived in a cave for one hundred days and ate only mugwort and garlic, they would become women.

The bear succeeded, and the god rewarded her with a human body. Together, they created the Korean people.

But the tiger was impatient. She wouldn't deal with those conditions. She ran out of the cave and was doomed to a life of stalking through the forest as a beast, alone.

I'd known about the bear-woman, but until then I'd never heard about the tiger. And yet in my draft, I'd written about a tiger-girl who asks a sky god to turn her human. The words had felt right when I wrote them, though I didn't quite understand them.

Now, *this* felt like more than a coincidence.

Yes—maybe I'd heard the story before, and it had burrowed, long forgotten, in my subconscious. But all the same, I felt connected to something bigger. I felt the way I had so many years earlier, as if these stories lived in my blood, even the ones I'd never heard before.

I dug deeper into the myth and found a critical essay called "Begetting the Nation," by Seungsook Moon. According to Moon, "the transformation of a bear into a woman carries the deep social meaning of womanhood epitomized by patience to endure suffering and ordeal."*

And with that, my story finally fell into place.

Here was the secret history. Because if the bear represents Korean women—or a version of womanhood that means suffering and silent endurance—what, then, of the tiger?

What about the woman who refused to suffer and was banished for it?

What would happen if she came back?

What would she want—and what story would she tell?

---

* Seungsook Moon, "Begetting the Nation," in *Dangerous Women: Gender & Korean Nationalism,* eds. Elaine H. Kim and Chungmoo Choi (New York: Routledge, 1998), 41.

Acknowledgments

This is the book I knew I had to write, but didn't know how. It's the product of so many wrong turns; of false starts (and false endings, and false middles); of sweat, tears, and tiger blood. But it's here. It's *done.* And I'm so grateful to everyone who helped along the way.

Mom: Thank you for planting the seed way back When Tiger Smoked His Pipe. For reading every single draft, thinking it through beat by beat, and talking me out of quitting (at least five times). This book would not exist without you. You are the best editor, the best writer, the *best* best mom.

Dad: Thank you for teaching me to work hard and treat myself with respect. For walking me through taxes and Dale Carnegie and showing me that I am not only an artist but a professional, too. Your encouragement means so much to me.

Sunhi, my fierce tiger sister, with so much heart: Much of this story is the story of our family. So much of the writing process has meant learning who we are and where we come from. And when you take your own journey through our history and your identity—when you take all that love and turn it into dance magic—I'll be there, cheering you on, watching with awe.

Halmoni: Thank you for all your stories; they could fill infinite novels.

To my huge, loving, incredible extended family: Thank you for your support. I am so lucky.

To the wonderfully supportive Paleys and Nadels: How happy I am to be part of your family.

And Josh, always: Thank you for drying my tears at every roadblock and making me laugh again. Thank you for believing in me when I didn't believe in myself. And for helping me believe that I can be special.

Sarah Davies: Thank you so much for your support throughout the process. Thank you for seeing the potential in a kernel of an idea.

And thank you to the rest of the Greenhouse Team, and the Rights People, for all your hard work.

Chelsea Eberly: Thank you for putting up with my long emails that boiled down to *"AHH, HELP!"* and for insisting that this book was *not,* in fact, broken. Thank you for pushing me to do my best work and for helping me unlock my heart story.

Thank you also to the warm, passionate, and hard-working team at Random House Children's Books: Michelle Nagler, Barbara Bakowski, Katrina Damkoehler, Ken Crossland, Tracy Heydweiller, Jenna Lettice, Kelly McGauley, Adrienne Waintraub, Lisa Nadel, Kristin Schulz, Jillian Vandall, Emily Bamford, Julie Conlon, Sydney Tillman, Stevie Durocher, Emily Petrick, Shaughnessy Miller, Andrea Comerford, Emily Bruce, Cynthia Mapp, and more.

Thank you to Jedit for the gorgeous cover art.

Thanks to the students at Oceanside Middle School, Punahou School, and Kaimuki Middle School for helping me pick my title.

Big thanks to Kay Junglen and her team of readers at Sherrill-Kenwood library.

To Romily Bernard for reading and for offering encouragement when I desperately needed it.

To Sam Morgan for all your enthusiasm. The only reason I don't use your titles is because they are *too* good.

And to the friends who let me go on (and on) about this book—who offered pep, advice, support, distraction, tissues, and tea—I am beyond grateful.

Lastly, to the reader: This book has come so far and finally found its way to you. Thank you for giving it a home. This story is yours now.

About the Author

TAE KELLER was born and raised in Honolulu, where she grew up on purple rice, Spam musubi, and her halmoni's tiger stories. After high school, she moved in search of snow, and now lives in New York City. She is also the author of *The Science of Breakable Things*. Follow her monthly love letters at bit.ly/lovetae.

TaeKeller.com